SINS & NEEDLES

A Knitorious Murder Mystery

REAGAN DAVIS

COPYRIGHT

ISBN: 978-1-7772359-7-0 (ebook)

ISBN: 978-1-7772359-6-3 (print)

FOREWORD

Dear Reader,

Despite several layers of editing and proofreading, occasionally a typo or grammar mistake is so stubborn that it manages to thwart my editing efforts and camouflage itself amongst the words in the book.

If you encounter one of these obstinate typos or errors in this book, please let me know by contacting me at Hello@ReaganDavis.com.

Hopefully, together we can exterminate the annoying pests.

Thank you!

Reagan Davis

CONTENTS

CHAPTER 1

"I can't believe Claire Rivera will be here, in person! At our humble, little yarn store!" Marla claps her hands in front of her chin in delight. Her short, spikey pixie cut and brilliant blue eyes remind me of an excited elf.

My corgi, Sophie, jolts awake at the sound of Marla's clap, then realizing there's nothing to see here, lowers her head and resumes her nap.

Marla works part-time at my yarn store, Knitorious. Claire Rivera is her favourite author. Besides being the world-famous author of the hugely popular Familia series of books, Claire is also an avid needle felter and fellow fibre enthusiast. She's in town this week to attend Harmony Lake's annual Between the Covers Book Fair.

In honour of Claire's attendance at the book fair, our local Charity Knitting Guild needle felted miniature versions of the characters and settings from Claire's famous book series. They're selling the miniatures during the book fair and donating the proceeds to ABC Life Literacy Canada, a nonprofit organization that supports community-based literacy programs.

Claire learned about the charity knitters' initiative when an anonymous fan—me! I'm the anonymous fan—sent her a link to an article on The Front Page, Harmony Lake's online newspaper. She emailed me, asking if she could visit Knitorious after-hours to view the display in person. I replied, telling her I'm closing the store early today for a special reveal for the charity knitters who crafted the display, and suggested that she would be welcome to attend. She accepted my invitation. To protect her privacy, and prevent mass disappointment if she doesn't show up, I haven't told the charity knitters that Claire is attending. The only people who know are me, Connie, Marla, my best friend, April, and my boyfriend, Eric.

"How's that?" I ask, after placing the last character into the display.

"Oh, Megan, it's perfect!" Marla replies, her blue eyes sparkling. "Claire Rivera will love it!"

Until this week, I never noticed how often we refer to famous people by their first and last names as if it's one name.

"I certainly hope so," Connie interjects. "As a needle felter, Claire Rivera should appreciate the time and effort that went into this exhibit."

Needle felting is the process of repeatedly stabbing animal fibre with a barbed needle to manipulate the fibre into 3D sculptures. Each miniature character and object in our display took hours of work and thousands of stabs.

Connie is my other part-time employee and surrogate mother. Connie and I met when Adam, Hannah, and I first moved to Harmony Lake almost seventeen years ago. We became instant friends, and soon after, we became family. I lost my mum just after Hannah's first birthday, and Hannah was born when I was just twenty-one. So, when Connie and I met, I was a young, recently married, new mum who was grieving. I'd wandered into Knitorious to buy yarn because I had knitted through my entire yarn stash while knitting through my grief during Hannah's naps. Connie welcomed us, nurtured us, and filled the mother and grandmother-shaped holes in our hearts. At almost seventy-one years young, she's the most beautiful, smart, and sophisticated woman I know. Connie is the original owner of Knitorious. I started working for her part-time about six years ago. Last year, she decided it was time to retire and move out of the apartment above the store. She moved into a new condo with her boyfriend, Archie, and I took over as owner of Knitorious. So, now I own Knitorious, and Connie works for me part-time. We've come full circle.

"According to the Harmony Lake rumour mill, Claire Rivera has been in town for over a week already," Marla informs us, smoothing her salt-and-pepper pixie cut. "Rumour has it she and her assistant are staying in a rental cottage on the lake, and she's writing the next *Familia* book."

Most of that is probably true. The Harmony Lake rumour mill's remarkable accuracy rate is matched only by their speed and dedication.

"Has anyone seen her around town?" I ask.

"Not that I've heard," Marla responds, "but apparently, she's reclusive when she's working."

"Claire Rivera isn't the only celebrity in Harmony Lake this week," Connie reminds us. "I heard that Jules Janssen and her entourage booked an entire floor at King of the Hill."

Jules Janssen is an award-winning, A-list Hollywood actor. She's attending the Between the Covers Book Fair to sign copies of her autobiography, *Pretending to be Real: My Life as an Optical Delusion.*

King of the Hill is one of the two ski resorts in the Harmony Hills mountains. The mountains border our cozy town to the north, and the lake borders us to the south. Harmony Lake is a tiny patch of small-town paradise nestled snugly between a lake and a mountain range. The mountains keep us busy with tourists during the winter months, and the lake ensures we're overrun with tourists in the summer months.

"Why would she need an entire floor?" I wonder out loud.

Marla counts on her fingers and replies, "Her

manager, her agent, her publicist, her security team, her glam squad..."

"I get it," I say, nodding. "It takes a team of people for Jules Janssen to go anywhere." Great, now I'm referring to people by their first and last names too.

"This will be our biggest, most successful book fair ever. We've never had three celebrities before," Marla observes. "And none of them would be here if it weren't for you, Megan. I can't tell you how thankful the book club is."

"It was nothing," I reply. "I just made one phone call."

The book club worried the annual book fair would be a bust because Harmony Lake has had some less-than-positive publicity over the past year, thanks to a sudden surge in mysterious deaths. It scared the organizers that book lovers might skip Between the Covers in favour of book fairs hosted by towns with lower murder rates.

The organizing committee embraced the negative publicity and made murder mysteries and crime thrillers this year's book fair theme. To help make the book fair a success, I asked my father, famous mystery author Mitchell Monroe, to attend as a guest author and maybe do a reading and sign some books. My father, who loves to be the centre of attention everywhere he goes, graciously accepted the invitation. He and my stepmother, Zoe, are scheduled to arrive in Harmony Lake tomorrow.

I doubt he'll be as excited as Marla about two other celebrities; Mitchell likes to be the most famous person in whatever room he occupies.

"Well, because of your phone call, the other two celebrities came to us!" Marla sounds amazed. "First, Claire Rivera contacted us because she heard we scheduled Mitchell Monroe to attend, then Jules Janssen contacted us and asked if we could fit her in as a guest author. Can you imagine? A celebrity worried *we* might turn *them* away!"

"I'm looking forward to seeing Mitchell and Zoe again," Connie says, changing the subject. "I hope we're able to spend some quality time together between book fair engagements."

"We're having a family dinner on Saturday night," I remind her. "And I'm sure Mitchell and Zoe will make time for you. I think they come to Harmony Lake as much to visit you and Archie as they do to visit me and Hannah."

Hannah is my daughter. She's nineteen years old and attends university four and a half hours away in Toronto. Mitchell and Zoe are stopping in Toronto to visit Hannah on their way here. They're staying in Toronto overnight, then driving to Harmony Lake tomorrow morning.

"Well, I'm carrying around a few copies of the celebrity authors' books and a pen, so if I bump into them around town, I can ask them to sign them for me."

"That sounds heavy," I respond. "If I bump into one

of them, I guess I'll have to ask them to sign my e-reader," I joke.

While we tidy the store to prepare for the big needle-felting-reveal party and celebrity-author guest star, we gossip about the rumoured plot of Claire Rivera's next *Familia* book and the outlandish tabloid magazine stories about Jules Janssen's love life. Our conversation ends when the bell over the door jingles, and a customer enters the store.

"Hi, there," I greet the customer, smiling.

She acknowledges me with a tight-lipped smile. Sophie rushes from her bed to the door to greet the new arrival, but the customer either ignores or doesn't notice the corgi pacing at her feet trying to get her attention. Sophie finally gives up and jumps on the sofa in the cozy knitting area to lick her wounded pride.

She doesn't look familiar. But with her dark sunglasses and baseball cap pulled down over her eyes, it's hard to tell. She might be a tourist in town for the book fair.

I busy myself pushing a broom around the back half of the store, aware of the mystery shopper lingering nearby. She sneaks glances at me as she slowly wanders toward me. When I feel her gaze on me, I turn and she looks away. She pets the yarn like she's shopping for canned goods, not squishy, fluffy yarn. I don't think she's a fibre artist.

"Can I help you find anything?" I ask when she's about a metre away from me.

"Are you Megan Monroe?" The mystery shopper asks.

"I was. Once upon a time," I reply. "No one has called me that for over twenty years. Do we know each other?"

"I'm sorry." The mystery shopper shakes her head. "I wasn't sure. I couldn't find any information about you online. You're Mitchell Monroe's daughter, right?"

Great. She's a Mitchell Monroe fan. I bet she's here to ask me to help her meet my dad.

"Yes, Mitchell Monroe is my dad, but my name is Megan Martel," I explain. "Listen, if you're hoping to meet Mitchell, he's scheduled to read from his latest book…"

The mystery shopper waves her hands, interrupting me mid-sentence. "I'm not a fan," she elaborates. Then she chuckles. "I'm sorry, that sounded rude. I mean, I *am* a fan, I've read several of your father's books, but that's not why I'm here. I'm here to ask you a favour."

This piques my interest.

"What kind of favour?" I ask.

The mystery shopper takes off her sunglasses and baseball cap. She shakes out her thick, glossy, auburn hair and flashes me an impossibly white, toothy smile.

"You're Jules Janssen," I say, shocked and maybe a bit starstruck.

She nods. "Is there somewhere private where we can talk?" she asks, checking behind both shoulders for potential interlopers.

Why would an A-list celebrity look for information about me online? What kind of favour could she possibly want me to do for her? There's only one way to find out.

"Sure," I reply, "follow me." I jerk my head toward the back room.

CHAPTER 2

I GESTURE for Jules to go first, and as she steps in front of me, a finger taps my shoulder.

"Is that Jules Janssen?" Connie mouths, exaggerating her silent words to ensure I understand her.

"Yes," I mouth, nodding.

"What does she want?" Connie mouths, concern creasing her forehead and the corners of her blue eyes.

I shrug. "I don't know," I mouth. Then in my normal volume, I add, "Why don't you join us? I'm sure Marla can cope by herself for a few minutes."

Connie nods in agreement and slips past me into the back room.

Marla is busy making adjustments to the front display window and didn't seem to notice our incognito guest. I guess Jules's disguise works. I tell Marla that Connie and I will be back in a few minutes, and tell her to holler if she needs us.

Jules introduces herself to Connie, and I invite them to have a seat at the table in the kitchenette area. I offer Jules a tea or coffee, which she declines, and join them at the small table.

"I understand Claire Rivera is planning to visit your store this evening," Jules says.

"Where did you hear that?" I ask, neither confirming nor denying her statement.

"Irrelevant," Jules responds, waving away my comment. "I've been trying to meet with Claire for months. She won't take my calls or answer my emails. She's a hard person to get in touch with. I've resorted to following her to book fairs and book signings to get some face time with her."

"OK," I acknowledge with a one-shoulder shrug. "What does it have to do with me?"

"I'm hoping you'll give Claire a gift for me," Jules explains, unzipping her backpack and pulling out a gift bag with tissue paper artfully sticking out of the top.

"What is it?" I ask.

Jules Janssen might be famous, but I don't know her, and I'm not comfortable acting as a liaison between her and Claire. Especially if Claire has made it clear that she doesn't want to talk to Jules, and if I don't know what I'm passing along to Claire on Jules's behalf.

"Just a few small tokens," Jules replies. "I'll show you." She pulls the tissue paper out of the bag and places it on the table. "A copy of my autobiography, signed of course." She places the book on top of the tissue paper, flattening it, then she pulls out another book. "A popular needle felting book, signed by the author, with a personal inscription for Claire." She places the needle-felting book on top of her autobiography. "I had to pull a few strings to get this," she says, smiling and tapping the felting book. Jules reaches into the bag once more and pulls out a small felted sheep. "I needle felted this sheep myself. I learned how to needle felt to show Claire that I'm the perfect actor to play Mama in the film adaptations of the Familia book series."

The Familia book series tells the story of a modern-day organized crime family and their matriarch, Mama. Mama is a complex, interesting character. She's a loving mother, PTA member, and moral compass, but she's also a ruthless mob boss who will stop at nothing to protect her family and their interests. She's also a needle felter, and her needle felting acts as a plot device to show the reader how Mama feels; the more aggressively she stabs her current project, the angrier she is.

"I wasn't aware the Familia series is being made into a film," Connie says, excited at the prospect.

"It's not," Jules confirms, looking at Connie, "but I plan to change that." Jules looks at me. "I was born to play Mama," Jules insists. "I know Claire has said publicly that she'll never allow the books to be made into movies, but I know if I talk to her, I could change her mind."

"And you're hoping these gifts will convince her to talk to you?" I deduce.

Jules nods enthusiastically. "Exactly!" Her smile shows more teeth than I think I have in my entire mouth. "When she reads my autobiography, and this note I wrote to her,"—Jules opens the cover of the needle-felting book to reveal an envelope addressed to Claire in cursive handwriting—"I know she'll see I can help her bring *Familia* to life and introduce the series to a whole new audience."

I feel like she's trying to sell me something. This is definitely a practiced sales pitch.

I sigh. "If I see her," I disclaim, "I'll give Claire the gift bag, but I can't guarantee she'll contact you, or that she'll even open it."

"That's all I ask," Jules says, then she places her hand on top of mine. "Thank you, Megan! I appreciate it."

"No worries." I smile and drag my hand out from under hers.

"Also," Jules adds, lowering her chin and looking up at me coyly from beneath her long, well-maintained lash extensions. "I was hoping you could put in a kind word for me. Maybe you could say something like, I think Jules would be perfect for the role of Mama."

I don't like being manipulated.

"Jules," I say, sitting up a little straighter in my chair, "I'm happy to give the gift bag to Claire on your behalf, *if* I see her, but that's all I can do. Besides, I don't even know Claire, so my opinion won't mean anything to her."

"That's not what I hear," Jules responds matter-of-factly. "I'm told Claire and your father used to be very close. I'm sure it's not a coincidence that she's attending this book fair and visiting your store. I mean, you must be friends, otherwise why would an author as famous as Claire Rivera attend a book fair in this hick little town?" She chuckles, ignorant to the casual insult she just made.

I'm offended, and judging by the way Connie is smoothing her silver, chin-length bob with her chin held high, I'm not the only one.

Connie opens her mouth to speak, but I speak first, hoping to stop her from saying something she might regret. Connie is fiercely protective of the people she loves and of our sweet, tight-knit community. I think Jules Janssen just lost a fan.

"Like I said," I stand up, "I'll pass along the gift to Claire if I see her. If not, I'll leave it at the front desk at your hotel." Following my lead, Connie and Jules also stand up.

Connie opens the door that separates the back room from the store. "It was lovely to meet you, Ms. Janssen. I hope you enjoy your stay in our hick little town," she says in an over-the-top, saccharine-like voice with a fake smile plastered on her face.

"It was lovely to meet you, too, Connie," Jules responds, seemingly oblivious to Connie's intended sarcasm. "Here," she says, thrusting a business card at me. "This is my private number. Call or text me if Claire says anything at all about my gift, a potential movie, anything."

I take the card and smile. Jules gathers her auburn tresses and twists them into a bun, which she covers with her baseball cap. Then she dons her sunglasses and tugs the brim of the cap to shield her face. She hoists her backpack onto her shoulders.

"Have a nice day," I say.

Jules walks briskly toward the front of the store with her head down.

I gesture for Connie to exit the back room ahead of me, but she closes the door, places her hands on her slim hips, and quirks an eyebrow.

"Claire Rivera used to be close to your father?" Connie asks. "Neither you nor Mitchell have mentioned this before."

"Actually," I say, securing Jules's business card to the side of the fridge with a magnet, "we told you. We just didn't use Claire's name." I resume my seat at the table in the kitchenette.

"I'm listening, my dear," Connie says, taking the seat across from me.

"Remember about ten years ago when my dad's author assistant resigned out of nowhere, then became an overnight sensation with a book series that my dad swears was his idea?"

Connie nods, then gasps when the realization hits

her. "You don't mean Claire Rivera is the assistant who stole Mitchell's idea?"

I nod. "That's what my dad says. He swears the Familia series was his idea. He hadn't written any books, but the series was in the development stage, and he had made extensive notes when Claire quit. Then less than a year later, out of nowhere, she hit the best-seller lists with the first *Familia* book."

"Why didn't Mitchell do something?" Connie asks. "Couldn't he have sued her or something?"

"He considered it," I admit, "but he didn't want to give her any more oxygen, as he likes to say. He believes there's no such thing as bad publicity, and he didn't want to help make Claire's series more popular than it already was. Also, he didn't want to appear bitter, like he resented his former assistant's success. He confronted her privately, but she denied it. So, he did nothing. He kept writing his books and moved on with his life."

"Does Claire know you own Knitorious?" Connie asks. "Is she coming tonight intentionally to see you, or will she be shocked you're here?"

I shrug and shake my head. "I don't know. I've been asking myself the same questions. She emailed me at the store email address, but when I replied, I signed the email, Megan Martel. She knows my dad is attending the book fair. Back in the day, before my father accused her of plagiarism, she knew I lived in Harmony Lake. Claire and I were never close, but we were friendly. We haven't spoken since she resigned as my dad's author assistant."

"It sounds like tonight might be more interesting than we were expecting," Connie observes.

We stop talking when someone knocks on the door. Marla opens the door enough to peek her head in.

"I'm sorry to interrupt, ladies."

"You're not interrupting anything, Marla," I assure her.

"Megan and I were just talking about the book fair," Connie adds.

"Would one of you mind standing on the sidewalk and telling me if the book fair banner in the display window is straight and centred?" Marla asks.

"Of course," I reply, standing up.

"Megan, you take the sidewalk, and I'll help Marla in the window," Connie instructs.

Stepping onto the sidewalk, I squint into the midday sun. I should've grabbed my sunglasses. I position myself on the curb and use one hand as a visor to keep the sun out of my eyes as I squint at the store window.

I use my free hand to point to my left. "To the left," I shout, even though they can't hear me.

Marla and Connie nod, then move the banner to the left.

"Stop," I shout, holding up my hand in a stop motion. They stop, and I give them a thumbs-up.

I point to the right, then jerk my thumb upward. The right side needs to move up a little. Marla complies, and I wave when she raises it enough. Then I give them another thumbs-up.

I'm about to go inside when something catches my eye. In the blur of my peripheral vision, something moves around the corner, in the laneway that leads to the parking lot, behind the store. I check for traffic, then step backward, off the curb, and onto Water Street. I crane my neck and squint, trying to peek around the corner. It's Jules Janssen. The back of her baseball cap and backpack are facing me. She's not alone. A younger, well-dressed, bald man stands in front of her. They're stance is intimate and friendly, and they're in each other's personal space. He's smiling and laughing. He's handsome. His hand moves to her butt, further convincing me they're more than friends. He stoops down and kisses her. Yup, definitely more than friends.

If someone told me this morning that I'd catch A-list celebrity Jules Janssen canoodling with a tall, handsome stranger in the alley beside my store, I would have said they were crazy, but here we are.

CHAPTER 3

MARLA AND CONNIE go home to freshen up before they meet their favourite author, and I sit down at the harvest table near the back of the store and work on a miniature, needle-felted Sophie. It's for my daughter, Hannah. I plan to turn it into a key chain and give it to her when she comes home for the summer in a couple of weeks.

Stabbing is oddly satisfying; nothing relieves stress like stabbing something over-and-over with a sharp, barbed needle.

The bell over the door jingles, bringing me back to reality.

"Megastar, where are you?"

My best friend, April, likes to call me nicknames that are puns of my name. Today, I'm Megastar.

"I'm here," I say on my way to the counter.

April places a large, white confectionery box on the

counter, and we have a tight hug. Then she squats down to greet Sophie, who's acting like she might explode if April doesn't acknowledge her right now.

"The needle-felting display looks amazing," she says.

"Thank you," I respond. "We worked hard on it. There are a lot of bandaged fingers in Harmony Lake this week because of this display," I tease, referring to all the crafters who accidentally stabbed themselves instead of the fibre.

"Are you ready for Claire Rivera's visit?" April asks, using Claire's first and last name.

I nod. "As ready as we can be. I'm waiting until the last minute to put out the finger food." I point to the confectionery box with the Artsy Tartsy logo on the lid. "What's this?"

April and her wife, Tamara, own the local bakery, Artsy Tartsy. Tamara is a talented pastry chef, and her creations are famous around here.

"A little something for your event," April replies.

She opens the box to reveal cookies shaped like stacks of book spines. Tamara used icing to make the book spines look like the Familia series of books. She captured the colours, titles, and even the font with perfection.

"Oh, April!" I gasp in disbelief at the artistry. "Please tell T she's outdone herself. These are beautiful!" I resist the urge to pick one up.

T is what we call Tamara.

"She wanted to do something special," April explains. "We'll be selling these, along with other bookish treats, during the book fair."

"These will take centre stage on the table," I declare, carrying the box to the harvest table.

I tidy my needle-felting supplies and head to the kitchenette in search of a platter to display the cookies.

"Has Claire confirmed she's still coming?" April asks, following me into the kitchenette.

I shake my head. "No, but she hasn't backed out, either, so I assume she'll be here."

"Do you think it will be weird?" she asks. "Because of her history with your dad? I can be here if it'll help," she offers.

"That's sweet." I smile. "But I know you and T are working all hours baking for the book fair. I'll be fine on my own. Besides, Connie knows about Claire and Mitchell's history, so if I need support, she'll have my back."

I find the platter I'm looking for; it's in the cabinet above the fridge. Seeing me struggle on my tippy toes, my tall best friend reaches above the fridge with little effort and retrieves it for me.

"Thank you for helping your short friend," I joke.

April and I are opposites in more than height. Where she's tall and willowy, I'm short and curvy. Where she has straight, blonde hair, I have long, curly, brown hair. April has blue eyes and a year-round tan, whereas I have hazel eyes and fair skin.

"What you lack in height, you make up for in personality, Megapop," April reassures me. "Anyway, you're in good company. T is friends with the chef at King of the Hill, and he said Jules Janssen is shorter in person than on the big screen. She's about your height. Good things come in small packages."

"He's right," I agree. "She is my height. I didn't realize it until you mentioned it."

"How do you know how tall Jules Janssen is?" April asks, her eyes narrow.

"I met her today," I reply. "She came to the store incognito."

"Spill!" April demands.

While we plate the bookish cookies, then plate and arrange the rest of the food, I tell April about my discussion with Jules, the gifts she wants me to give to Claire, and her cozy conversation with the unknown man in the alley beside Knitorious.

"If Jules's plan works, and Claire agrees to talk to her because of you, you'll be able to say you're the reason they made the *Familia* books into movies," April theorizes. "Maybe they'll include your name in the credits."

"As what?" I ask. "Artist liaison? Mutual acquaintance? Small-town hick?"

April stops plating finger sandwiches and looks at me. "Small-town hick?"

I tell April about Jules's offhand remark about Harmony Lake, and I think Jules just lost another fan.

We finish plating the cheese and crackers, and the bell over the door jingles. Connie, Marla, and a handful of charity knitters enter the store together.

"I have to go," April whispers. She stands up and pushes in her chair. "Text me if you need anything. I can be here in less than five minutes. Two if it's for drama."

I nod. "I will."

April gives me a smile and says hi and bye to everyone on her way out.

AFTER THE LAST charity knitter arrives, I lock the door and replace the OPEN sign with the CLOSED FOR A PRIVATE FUNCTION sign we hardly ever have occasion to use.

I make the rounds, greeting each person and thanking them for coming. Then, while everyone exchanges compliments, admiring the display and each other's needle-felting prowess, I slip into the kitchen to make tea and coffee.

While putting coffee and tea condiments on a tray, a dull thud at the back door gets my attention. Not a knock, more like a kick.

"Hello?" I say through the closed door.

"Hello?" a woman's voice replies, sounding strained. "A little help?"

"Oh, my goodness!" I say when I open the door to a young, blonde, full-figured woman who's buckling under the weight of a cardboard box. "Let me help," I insist. "You've really got your hands full."

"Careful, it's heavy." The mystery woman grunts as we ease the box from her arms to mine. "Thank you," she says with a heavy sigh. "As much as I love books, they're heavy when you pack lots of them in the same box." She chuckles.

I place the box on the table in the kitchenette. "I didn't order any books," I say, confused and wondering if she's delivering them to the wrong store.

"Claire brought them for the needle felters who made the *Familia* display," she explains. "They're signed. We weren't sure how many to bring, and we probably brought too many."

"Oh," I say, struck with comprehension. "You're with Claire!" I smile. "Hi! I'm Megan Martel. It's nice to meet you." I extend my hand.

"Dina Langley," she responds, shaking my hand. "Claire Rivera's assistant."

"Will Claire be joining us, or are you here on her behalf?" I ask, pouring water from the kettle to the teapot.

"Claire's in the car. She's finishing a call. She'll be right in," Dina replies. "I hope it's all right to use the back door. I don't think I could carry that box around to the front."

"Of course," I assure her. "I'm glad I was nearby to hear you knock—er, kick."

I pick up the tray of tea and condiments to carry

them to the harvest table in the store, with the finger food.

"Let me take that for you," Dina suggests. She's already taking the tray from me before she finishes her sentence. "I'm dying to see the display." Her smile is genuine and warm.

"Oh, do you needle felt?" I ask, letting go of the tray.

"No." She shakes her head. "But I've watched Claire do it, and I admire the creativity and skill. The little forest animals are my favourite. I think they're adorable."

A sharp rap at the back door brings an abrupt end to our conversation. On my way to open it, I tell Dina where to put the tray, thank her for her help, and tell her to help herself to the refreshments.

I take a deep breath and brace myself to see Claire for the first time in a decade. For the first time since she betrayed my father.

"Megan." Claire's smile is warm but cautious. "Do you remember me? Claire Rivera? I was Mitche..."

"Of course, I remember you, Claire!" I smile and she pulls me into an awkward hug. "You look the same as you did ten years ago. Why haven't you aged?" I ask when I pull away.

It must be the dimples; For whatever reason, dimples make people look younger. At thirty-five, Claire is six years younger than me, but she doesn't look a day over twenty-five. It helps she has ageless features; her large brown eyes, round face, and dimpled cheeks suggest youth. She styles her brown hair the same, just below her shoulders with bangs. Claire Rivera looks exactly as I remember.

"I was about to ask you the same question," she replies. "You're radiant."

"Thank you," I say.

"How's Hannah?" she asks.

I pull my phone from my pocket and open the camera roll. "You might regret asking that," I tease.

Claire and I spend a few minutes getting caught up. She moved to the West Coast after she resigned as my father's assistant, and she never married because *Familia* takes up most of her life. I sense a hint of resentment in her voice when she talks about how much of her life she devotes to her book series. I show her more pictures of Hannah than she needs to see and tell her about the divorce. Our interaction is less awkward than I expected, and I sense Claire feels the same way; our mutual relief is palpable.

"I'm sad I won't see Hannah while I'm here," Claire says. "But I'm glad she's doing well at university."

Behind Claire's back, Connie pops her head into the room and arches her brows, giving me a look that asks if everything is OK. I smile at her and subtly nod.

"I hope we can get together and catch up while you're in town," I say, "but I think you should make an appearance in the store before the charity knitters accuse me of keeping you to myself."

"Of course," Claire says. "Where's Dina?" She looks

around the small room. "We'll need her to carry the books." She points at the box on the table.

"I'll carry the books," I offer.

When Claire enters the room, the collective gasp from the charity knitters sounds like we're deflating a giant air mattress in the store. Within seconds, Claire's fans surround her, clamouring to be next to introduce themselves and shake her hand.

I place the books near the door, so each guest can take one when they leave. When I stand up, I notice the top of Dina's head near the floor, behind the sofa, and in front of the display window.

"Are you OK?" I ask, approaching her.

"We're fine!" Dina flashes me a wide grin and looks up at me from the floor where she sits cross-legged with Sophie's head resting in her lap. "I'm not antisocial," she explains. "I just love dogs. And this one is so sweet that I can't stop rubbing her."

"Yes, she is," I agree. "Her name is Sophie, and she's allowed on the furniture. It might be more comfortable for you than the hardwood floor." I gesture to the two sofas in the cozy knitting area.

"I should socialize with the humans," Dina says. Then she looks at Sophie. "I'm sorry, Sophie, I have to do people things. I'll rub you again before I leave."

I extend my hand to help her up, and she accepts it.

"Nice unicorns," I say, pointing to the pink and purple unicorn bandage on Dina's index finger.

"Thanks," she laughs. "The first aid kit at our rental

cottage has an eclectic collection of supplies. The only bandage options are unicorns or jack-o'-lanterns, and since it's April, I went with the unicorns." She shrugs.

"If it's serious, there's a walk-in medical clinic over…"

"It's not," Dina interrupts, flicking her wrist. "It's a paper cut. Occupational hazard in my job."

Through the display window, I spy the handsome, well-dressed, bald man who was kissing Jules Janssen earlier. He is pacing on the sidewalk across the street.

Noticing my distraction, Dina asks me what's wrong.

"That man," I say, nodding toward the display window. "Have you seen him before?"

Dina's eyes follow my gaze. "Brooks?" she asks. "The bald guy in the expensive suit?"

"You know him?" I ask.

She nods. "His name is Brooks Wiley. He's Claire's literary agent."

"Really?" I ask, wondering if he's the reason Jules knew about Claire's visit to Knitorious today.

Why would Brooks Wiley sneak around town, making out with Jules Janssen, someone his client is trying to avoid?

Duh! Why wouldn't he? She's Jules Janssen, recipient of Hollywood's most-beautiful-person-in-the-world-award.

"Why do you ask?"

I shake my head. "No reason," I reply. "He was

hanging around outside earlier, and I've never seen him before. Tourists don't dress like that or look so intense."

"That's just Brooks," she assesses flippantly. "He's made of expensive Italian suits and smoldering intensity."

"Brooks is welcome to come in," I offer. "He doesn't have to wait for you and Claire outside."

"I don't think he's waiting for us," she says. "I don't know why he's there. Trust me, if he wanted to come in, he would."

Her last sentence sounds ominous.

I can't tell if Dina likes Brooks Wiley, but something about him makes me cautious, like I need to be hyper-aware of my surroundings when he's around.

CHAPTER 4

Claire inspects the needle-felting display, strolling from item to item with her hands clasped behind her back, smiling and dispensing generic compliments as she saunters past each piece of the exhibit. She reminds me of the parent volunteers who judged the science fair exhibits when Hannah was in elementary school.

A few paces behind her, Dina pets each miniature person, place, and animal. She marvels at the accuracy of each tiny character and setting from the books.

"There's even a miniature Mama needle felting in her easy chair!" she proclaims with awe.

With unbridled enthusiasm, Dina asks who made each item, then compliments their workmanship.

While everyone is busy hovering around the exhibit, waiting their turn for Claire and Dina to compliment their creative talent, Connie and I slip away to the kitchenette to refresh the tea and coffee and fill the water pitcher.

"Is it me, or does Claire Rivera seem... I don't know"—Connie tosses her hand in the air—"indifferent to the exhibit?"

"It's not you," I assure her, plugging in the kettle. "I noticed it too. She's kind of standoffish."

"And she has touched nothing! My dear, have you ever encountered a fibre artist who doesn't squish the fibre?"

I shake my head. "I noticed that too," I concur. "Maybe she keeps her hands clasped behind her back to avoid touching it. Maybe she's afraid she'll break something, or doesn't want to touch it without buying it?" I venture a guess at some unlikely reasons to explain Claire's apparent apathy toward the craft she claims to love.

When we emerge from the kitchenette, Claire's inspection of the exhibit is over, and several knitters are milling around the harvest table, *oohing* and *aahing* over the bookish cookies from Artsy Tartsy. Dina is in the thick of it, taking selfies with the cookies and crafters.

Where's Claire? I scan the store and find her near the counter, looking disinterested as she thumbs through a book of knitting patterns, licking the tip of her thumb and index finger before each page turn.

I place a bookish cookie on a plate, grab a napkin, and join her.

"Our local pastry chef made these in your honour," I say, placing the plate and napkin on the counter.

"How clever," she comments, looking at the cookie and smiling.

"Would you mind if I took a photo of you holding the cookie?" I ask. "She's a dear friend, and it would mean a lot to her to have a picture of you with one of her creations."

"Of course!" Claire uses the napkin to pick up the cookie and holds it next to her cheek. She smiles and raises her eyebrows, moving her eyeballs toward the cookie without turning her head.

"Perfect," I say, snapping two photos. "Thank you, Claire."

"No problem," she says, then looks at her watch. "We should get going."

Claire stares at Dina until Dina makes eye contact with her. Claire winks and smiles at Dina before she resumes thumbing through the book, licking her thumb and index finger before turning the page.

Was that a wink, or a wink? Is Dina more than Claire's author assistant?

"Claire," I whisper. "Are you and Dina a couple?"

"What?" she asks, her face scrunched up with confusion. "No! Why would you ask that?"

"I'm sorry," I atone. "It's the wink. I couldn't tell if it was a friendly wink or a flirty wink," I explain. "It's none of my business. Please don't feel compelled to answer me. If you are a couple, Dina is super nice, and I hope you're happy."

Claire laughs and closes the pattern book, pushing it aside. "Dina and I aren't a couple, Megan," she informs me. "Our relationship is purely professional. She's my assistant, nothing more. We're barely friends, for goodness' sake. The wink is how I signal to Dina that I want to leave in five minutes."

"Ohhh," I respond. "That's smart."

Claire continues to chuckle under her breath and points toward the harvest table. "I'm going to say goodbye and thank everyone," she says.

I do a headcount of the felters. Twelve. I remove twelve books, then carry the box to the back room, place it on the floor near the back door, and place Jules's gift bag on top.

Standing in the doorway to the back room, I listen as Marla, on behalf of the book club and the charity knitters, thanks Claire and Dina for attending the book fair and gracing us with their presence at Knitorious this afternoon. Accompanied by applause, Claire and Dina retreat to the back room.

"What's this?" Claire asks, nodding at Jules's gift on top of the book box.

"It's a gift for you from Jules Janssen," I start. "I'm sorry. I'm not comfortable with this, and I understand if you don't want to accept it. Jules asked me to give it to you on her behalf."

Claire rolls her eyes, then looks at Dina, and they both laugh, shaking their heads.

"Unbelievable," Claire says, then she touches my arm. "Megan, I'm sorry Jules put you in the middle like this. She's been harassing me for months to sell her the movie rights to *Familia*."

"She mentioned that," I say.

"Well, she's wasting her time," Claire asserts. "The only way *Familia* will become a movie or TV series is over my dead body." She looks at Dina and points to the box and gift bag. "Take these to the car, Dina. I'll meet you there."

Dina nods, and stoops to pick up the box.

"It was nice to meet you, Dina," I say, holding the door open for her.

"You too, Megan," she smiles. "Maybe we'll see each other at the book fair."

"Megan, before I leave, can I ask you something?" Claire asks, scanning the room to make sure we're alone.

"Does Mitchell still hate me?"

That's a big question, and not one I'm qualified to answer.

"To be honest, Claire, I'm not sure how my dad feels about you. He hasn't mentioned you in years."

"That could mean anything," she surmises. "Maybe he hates me more than ever, maybe he's forgiven me."

I purse my lips into a tight line and shrug. I don't know what to say. "Your guess is as good as mine."

"I want you to know that I didn't steal *Familia* from Mitchell. I didn't know what he was working on when I resigned. I never had access to his works-in-progress. And I would never hurt him. Your father is a brilliant, creative author, and I learned so much from him. He's my mentor. I left because I felt it was time for me to stretch my creative wings. I was afraid if I didn't do it then, I never would. But I swear to you, I plagiarized nothing of Mitchell's."

"OK." I hope she's not looking to me for forgiveness because it's not my place to offer it.

"Do you think you could arrange a meeting between Mitchell and me while we're both in Harmony Lake?" Claire asks.

"*Ooof,*" I sigh. "I'm not sure, Claire," I reply, shaking my head. "I can ask him, but I don't know if he'll be open to it. What do you want from him?"

"Nothing," she replies. "I want to explain why I left and assure him I didn't steal his idea. I don't expect us to be friends, but it would be nice if we weren't enemies. I'm ready to write the next chapter of my life, and I'd like this chapter to end with no loose ends." She reaches into her pocket and produces a business card. "Contact me if Mitchell agrees." She hands me the card. "This has my contact information and Dina's. Be sure to contact me. Dina is my assistant, and I keep my professional and personal lives separate."

"OK," I respond. "I'll tell my dad you want to bury

the hatchet." I add Claire's card to the fridge, under the same magnet as Jules's card.

"I hope Mitchell wants to bury the hatchet too," Claire says, opening the back door. She chuckles. "I just hope he doesn't want to bury it in my head."

CHAPTER 5

Thursday, April 15th

Hannah: Grandma and Grandpa just left. They said to tell you they'll be in Harmony Lake by dinner. Followed by an old-man emoji, old-woman emoji, and car emoji.

Me: OK. Thanks. Good luck on your exam! Followed by a shamrock emoji and heart emoji.

Hannah: And Grandpa said to tell Dad the books will be delivered to his office today. Followed by a book emoji, heart emoji and several cardboard-box emojis.

Adam: Thanks, Princess! Good luck with your exam. Followed by a crossed-fingers emoji and a one-hundred-percent emoji.

"Are you going to text Mitchell and tell him the books arrived?" Adam asks after he hits send on his text to the chez Martel group chat with him, Hannah, and me.

"There's no point. He and Zoe turn off their phones when they're in the car." I shrug. "I texted the person who sent them from the publisher and told her they arrived."

Adam is my ex-husband. He's also the mayor of Harmony Lake and our town's only lawyer. After twenty years of marriage, we finalized our divorce last year. As far as divorces go, ours was as amicable as it gets. We worked hard to keep our family intact, and we always put our daughter first. Some days are easier than others, but we've redefined our relationship and remain friends. We love each other, but not how married people should; we aren't a couple anymore, but Adam and I will always be family.

We met in university when I was eighteen years old. We got married when I was twenty, and I became pregnant with Hannah a few months later. Adam was an ambitious workaholic who spent most of his time climbing the corporate ladder to senior partner, at a law firm in the city. I focused on raising Hannah and immersing myself in the community. Our marriage didn't have a dramatic ending. It fizzled out. Neither of us noticed until it was too late; one day we realized the only thing we had left in common was Hannah. After a few failed attempts to rekindle our connection, we decided it would be best for everyone to end our marriage.

"Why did your father have his books delivered to *my* office, anyway?" Adam asks. "Why didn't he send them to Knitorious since you're hosting his book signing?"

"He worried the delivery person would leave them in the parking lot, and Connie and I would have to lug them into the store," I explain. "He figured you'd transfer them from your office and do the lugging for us. I didn't know the books were being delivered to your office until after he shipped them. Otherwise, I would have asked him to send them here."

Adam's short, dark hair is coiffed into place and doesn't move when he shakes his head. "He did it to get under my skin, Meg. Mitchell's always trying to antagonize me." He hoists another box of books onto the harvest table. "He's trying to get a reaction out of me. To goad me into freaking out so I'll look crazy." Adam shakes his head again. "I won't give him the satisfaction."

"Who's trying to get a reaction out of you?" Eric asks, the sleeves of his shirt stretching under the pressure of his biceps as he heaves two more boxes onto the crowded table.

Adam tells Eric his theory that my father's mission in life is strategizing covert ways to torment him.

Eric is my boyfriend. He's also our local police chief and my tenant. He lives in the apartment above Knitorious, though we're renovating my house so he can move in with me. Living together is a big step for me, so Eric is moving in slowly. He stays at his apartment about fifty percent of the time and at chez Martel the other fifty percent. Chez Martel is what we call my house.

"Brace yourself, dude, Mitchell hates all his sons-in-law," Adam warns Eric. "But he hates me the most," he adds, sounding almost proud of his position as the least-liked son-in-law.

By all his sons-in-law, Adam is referring to himself, and my sister's current and former husbands.

"Adam, stop scaring him," I say, referring to Eric. "You're being dramatic. My dad is always cordial and courteous to you."

"That's part of his strategy, Meg," Adam argues, furrowing his thick brows over his blue eyes. "He manifests his hatred passive-aggressively so I can't confront him without looking paranoid." He looks at Eric. "Guess how many times Mitchell has killed me?" The look on Eric's face is blank, and he blinks. "Go on, guess," Adam urges.

"Mitchell killed you?" Eric asks, confusion clouding his handsome, chiseled face.

"Nineteen times," Adam replies, over-enunciating each syllable. "He always revives me so he can kill me again." The look of concerned confusion on Eric's face deepens. "You know Mitchell's Shark Attack book series?" Adam asks.

"I love those books," Eric replies, his concerned expression replaced by a more enthusiastic one. "I've read the entire series. It's one reason I wanted to be a cop." Comprehension flashes in his brown eyes.

"Wait!" he says, pointing at Adam. "Are you *The Shark*?"

Adam nods and smiles, looking proud of his self-appointed status as my father's favourite murder victim.

Mitchell Monroe's most popular book series is the Shark Attack series. The good guy is a cop named Rock Granite who devotes his life to apprehending a lawyer named Alan Mandell, a serial killer known as The Shark. In each book, Rock hunts The Shark. At the end, when Rock is about to capture him, The Shark fakes his own death; there's never a body. In the next book, The Shark, miraculously resurrected, kills again, Rock hunts him again, and he fakes his death again. Lather, rinse, repeat. Adam believes The Shark, Alan Mandell, is him, Adam Martel. My father insists it's a coincidence and says Adam shouldn't flatter himself.

I roll my eyes. "Don't listen to him," I tell Eric. "He's worried Mitchell will hate you more, and you'll replace him as most-hated son-in-law."

Instead of laughing at my attempt to make light of the situation, Eric looks worried. He furrows his brow, and his brown eyes dart back and forth between me and Adam.

"I'm joking," I assure him. "Mitchell will love you."

"You'll know in a few months," Adam warns. "If he hates you, Mitchell will write you into his next book and kill you."

Thanks for your support, Adam.

"Let's get the last few boxes from your car," Eric says, nudging Adam and changing the subject.

"You can hide at my condo until he leaves town," Adam mumbles to Eric as they leave the store. "I've got your back, dude."

"That won't be necessary," I call after them.

Yes, my ex-husband and boyfriend are friends. Good friends. Eric was new in town and didn't have any friends here. Despite living in Harmony Lake most of his adult life, Adam didn't have many relationships here because he'd spent all his time at his office in the city. They bonded over a mutual love of golf and Buffalo wings and became buddies. Is it weird to watch my boyfriend and ex-husband hang out? Yes, but no weirder than the friendship I have with Adam's new partner.

Our modern, non-traditional family is one example of the many families of choice in our quirky little town.

My dad sent too many books to display in the store. Adam clears yarn from the yarn shelves to make room to display some of them. Eric rearranges the storage room to accommodate the rest of the books and the displaced yarn. I erect an easel in the window to display the poster board of my Dad's picture, his latest book, and the time and date details of his appearance this Sunday.

I wrestle with the large, awkward cardboard poster while trying not to step on Sophie, who is napping in the sunny window. Connie is heading toward Knitorious, walking as fast as she can without breaking into a run.

Something's wrong. She's walking like she's on a mission. I lay the poster against the easel, sidestep the sleeping corgi, and squeeze out of the window. I rush to the door, open it, and with Sophie awake and now in tow, jog toward her, meeting her in front of the local deli.

"What's wrong?" I ask.

"Haven't you heard the news, my dear?" Connie asks, hooking her arm through mine and leading me toward Knitorious.

"What news?" I ask.

"Look at any of Claire Rivera's social media accounts," she instructs.

I pat my hip pockets. No phone. "My phone is in the store," I say, as we arrive at Knitorious. I open the door and make a beeline for the counter with my gaze locked on my phone. I unlock my phone, open the first social media app I see, and navigate to Claire's account. "Wow!" I gasp, bringing my hand to my mouth.

"What is it?" Adam asks from the bulky-yarn section where he's shelving *Shark Attack: Between A Rock and A Shark Place*, my dad's latest book.

"Claire Rivera is ending the Familia series," I reply.

Claire's social media post is short and to the point. It reads, "The next installment in the Familia series will be the last. It's time for me, Mama, and the rest of the

Familia to turn the page and start a new chapter. Thank you, dear readers, for ten wonderful years!"

"Why?" he asks, joining Connie and me at the counter. I hand him my phone so he can read Claire's social media post. "That's too bad," Adam says. "I love that series. I've read all the books."

"Think about the publicity her announcement will bring to the Between the Covers Book Fair," Connie adds. "People will flock here! They'll want to see Claire and get her to sign their books before she retires."

"She didn't say she's retiring," I point out.

Yesterday when she left, Claire told me she was ready to write the next chapter of her life and wanted to end this chapter with no loose ends. This must be what she meant.

We discuss the possibility that Claire's post is a publicity stunt, or that she's retiring the series in its current form but will continue it another way, like a spin-off series featuring another character, or a prequel series when my phone rings.

"It's Rick," I tell Connie and Adam. Rick Ransan is a local property investor. He owns a few lakeside rental cottages, including the one Claire Rivera and Dina Langley rented for their stay in Harmony Lake.

"Hello?"

"Megan? It's Rick. I'm trying to get in touch with Eric, but he's not answering my calls or texts." Besides a telltale echo that tells me Rick is calling from his car, there's a sense of urgency in his voice.

"He's here," I say. "Hang on, Rick, I'll get him for you."

I hustle to the storage room where Eric is shelving books and yarn.

"Rick is trying to reach you," I tell him. "It sounds important."

Eric pats his pockets. "My phone must be in the car."

I hand him my phone, and he puts it on speaker. I close the storage room door.

"Hey, Rick. It's Eric. What's up?"

"There's a problem at one of my rental cottages," Rick explains. "Someone locked themselves in the den. Her friend says the woman in the den isn't answering her phone and isn't answering when she knocks on the door."

"Did you call 9-1-1?" Eric asks.

"No," Rick replies. "The woman locked in the den is Claire Rivera. She was very specific when she rented the cottage that privacy is her biggest priority. I don't want to cause a big scene if she's having a nap or something. I'm on my way there with the spare key. Maybe you could meet me there. You know, just in case? Her friend sounds worried."

Eric nods, even though Rick can't see him.

"I'm on my way. Tell Megan the address. She'll text it to me in the car."

"If I get there before you, should I use my key to unlock the den door?" Rick asks.

"You won't get there before me," Eric says with confidence, then hands me the phone.

"Hang on, Rick." I put the call on hold.

"I'm sorry, babe, I have to deal with this. I'll be back as soon as I can to help you finish getting the store ready for your dad's book signing." He runs a hand through his short, brown hair.

"It's fine," I assure him. "Drive safe, please." I stand on my tippy toes and kiss him. "Let me know how it goes." I open the storage-room door.

"It's probably nothing," he says, hugging me and kissing the top of my head. "I'll be back before your dad and Zoe arrive. I want to make a good first impression."

"Stop worrying about that," I say.

Eric disappears out the back door, and I text him the address Rick gives me, then I look around, taking in the empty room. My eyes land on the business cards I stuck to the fridge yesterday. I take a photo of each card with my phone, then rip them up into tiny pieces, and drop the pieces in the recycling bin. I wouldn't want to be the reason some crazed fan gets hold of Jules Janssen's or Claire Rivera's contact information.

A WALL of warmth hits me when I open the door to Artsy Tartsy. The bakery always smells like warm, doughy bread and comfort.

"Hey, Megapop!" April greets me from behind the

counter. "Are you here to pick up your strawberry dream cake?" she asks.

I ordered a strawberry dream cake for dessert tonight. It's one of my dad and Zoe's favourite desserts.

I nod. "Yes, but will it keep until tomorrow? Dad and Zoe called, and they won't be here until tomorrow."

"It'll be fine. Keep it in the fridge," April replies. "Are Mitchell and Zoe all right?" There's a hint of concern in her voice.

"They're fine," I assure her. "My dad had a sudden surge of inspiration. They followed his muse off the highway to the nearest Wi-Fi signal so he could capture his ideas before they disappear. They don't like to drive at night, so they'll finish the drive to Harmony Lake tomorrow morning. Zoe said they found a hotel two hours south of here."

This is typical of my father. Adam likes to say Mitchell exists in his own time zone, MST: Mitchell Standard Time. He often shows up a day early or a day late. Time is something my father is not a slave to. Time and cell phones. He only turns on his phone when it's convenient for him, and he never turns it on when he's in the car because, according to him, some of his best ideas come to him when he's driving, and a ringing cell phone would scare away his muse.

"So, Eric gets to stay nervous about meeting your dad until tomorrow," April points out.

"I haven't told him yet. He went to work. Something

came up," I respond. "I don't know why he's so anxious." I shrug. "It must be because he's a fan of the Shark Attack series," I theorize.

"I think it's more than that, Megnolia," April says, as she boxes my cake. "He wants your dad to like him because he loves you. As far as Eric is concerned, he's meeting his future father-in-law. It wouldn't surprise me if Eric asks Mitchell for your hand in marriage," she teases. At least, I hope she's teasing.

"Whoa!" I raise my hands in a stop motion. "Settle down. I haven't even wrapped my head around moving in together yet. Anyway, who asks the bride's father for permission to propose nowadays? This isn't a Jane Austen novel." We laugh.

Eric wants us to get married, and so do I. Someday. There's no rush, and certainly no need for him to ask my father for permission. Some traditions are best left in the past.

I spy some fresh eclairs in the display. Adam and Connie's favourite. "Can you give me a few eclairs?" I ask, changing the subject. "Adam and Connie were amazing today. They helped me rearrange the store for Mitchell's book signing. The least I can do is thank them with treats."

While April boxes the eclairs, my phone rings.

"Eric," I tell her as I accept the call. "Hello?"

"Hey, babe. I'm sorry I haven't come back to help you at the store."

"It's OK," I assure him. "Police business is more important than a book signing."

Brief pause, followed by a sigh. "I don't think I'll make it home in time for dinner with your dad and Zoe. I'm sorry. Hopefully he understands."

"You won't miss dinner," I tell him. "They checked into a hotel for the night. They won't get here until tomorrow."

"Good." Another sigh, but this one is a sigh of relief. "This situation is more complicated than I expected. I'll be here for a while."

"Did you get into the den?" I ask. "Is she OK?"

"Yes, we got in, but she's not OK." Brief pause while Eric inhales a deep breath, then blows it out. "Claire Rivera is dead."

CHAPTER 6

"PARDON?" I ask, hoping I misheard him.

I didn't mishear him. Claire Rivera is dead.

"It's not public knowledge yet," Eric explains. "We still have to notify her family."

Another customer enters the bakery, so I wander to the back of the store.

"I understand," I whisper. "Does it look suspicious?"

"No, but we have to treat it as suspicious until the coroner determines otherwise," he reminds me. "I have to go. The coroner just got here. I love you."

"I love you too."

We end the call, and I stare at April as she serves her customer. She knows something is wrong just by looking at me. I don't need to say anything. April is my best friend. She can gauge my mood from what I say, what I don't say, my body language, the look on my face—heck, sometimes April knows how I feel before I know how I feel.

I can tell she's rushing through the transaction. She hands her customer their box of mini lemon pudding cakes, then hurries from behind the counter, beating her customer to the door. She holds the door for her customer, wishes them a good day, then locks it, and turns the sign from OPEN to CLOSED.

"What happened, Megabuck?"

Still in shock, I sit at one of the small bistro tables. April sits across from me.

"You can't say anything," I warn her. "It's a secret."

"Of course," April says. "You know I won't tell anyone."

I look around, despite knowing we're alone, except for Tamara, but she's in the kitchen and can't hear us. "Claire Rivera is dead," I whisper.

"What?" April asks, confused, like I broke into a foreign language mid-sentence.

I shrug. "I know. Unbelievable. Eric is there. He sounded just as shocked as we are."

"How?" she asks.

I shrug again. "I dunno, but he said it doesn't look suspicious."

Starting from Rick's urgent call to Eric about Claire locking herself in the den, I tell April everything.

"Her assistant must be beside herself," April says.

51

"I hadn't thought about Dina." A wave of guilt washes over me.

"Maybe you should go there and make sure she's OK," April suggests. "And I should go with you to make sure you're OK."

"We can't just show up at a crime scene," I argue. "No matter how tempted we are."

April shrugs one shoulder. "You've done it before," she points out.

"Because I was the person who found the body," I remind her. "This is different." Despite this, I'm searching for a reason to go there. "Without Claire, Dina is all alone." Found a reason!

"And she's not from here," April adds. "She doesn't know anyone in Harmony Lake, except for you."

"And she's a guest in our town," I continue. "We're a tight-knit, caring community. It would be neighbourly to check on her."

"Yes, it would," April agrees.

I remember the business card Claire gave me with her and Dina's contact information.

"I think I might have her cell number." I unlock my cell phone. "I can text her and offer to go there if she needs support," I propose as a compromise.

"Do it," April urges.

Me: Hi Dina. It's Megan Martel. Are you OK? I hear there's a commotion at your cottage.

Within seconds, three dots appear on the screen,

showing that Dina is typing a response. The three dots disappear, and my phone rings.

"It's her," I hiss.

"Answer it," April prompts.

I answer the call, and Dina is in hysterics. Her sobs make it difficult to understand what she's saying. I'm able to determine she's not allowed to go inside the cottage, but she's not allowed to leave. The police asked her a lot of questions but wouldn't answer the questions she asked them. Claire's family wants to talk to her, but the police asked her not to talk to them yet. They won't let her see Claire, and the police said she needs to find somewhere else to stay tonight.

"Oh, Dina, I'm so sorry," I say. My heart breaks for her. I know how scary it is to be at a death scene. "Is there anything I can do?"

"Ca-an you co-me he-re? Puh-lees? I do-n't kn-ow a-ny-one." She punctuates each syllable with the sharp intake of breath that accompanies hysterical sobbing.

"Of course," I say. "I'll be there as soon as I can."

I end the call, and April is already behind the counter boxing cookies.

"For the first responders," she explains. "And I'll bring a case of water too."

"I'll ask Connie to watch the store, and look after Sophie," I say. "Pick you up in ten minutes?"

My COMPACT SUV is a tight fit as I steer it along the long, winding, gravel driveway at the cottage. The emergency vehicles parked along the edges make the already narrow driveway even narrower. It's like driving through an obstacle course. About halfway up, I parallel park between two police cruisers, and we walk the rest of the way. April carries the cookies, and I carry the case of water.

If, like Rick said, privacy was Claire's priority, she chose the right cottage. We can't even see the cottage from where we parked. Thickets of century-old trees line both sides of the driveway and cottage, and the driveway is disguised as an unassumed road. If I didn't have GPS, I doubt I would've found the place.

At the top of the driveway, a uniformed officer stands guard.

"Uh-oh," April mutters. "Will he let us pass?"

"I think so," I reply. "I know him. He has a crush on Hannah. You offer cookies, I'll try to get us past him."

She nods in acknowledgement.

"Hi, Lucas," I say as we approach the young officer.

"Hi, Megan." He smiles. "That looks heavy. Let me help you." He jogs over and relieves me of the case of water.

"Thank you," I say, smiling. "We brought them for you and the other responders. If you have to stay at your post, I can deliver them," I offer.

"Cookie?" April smiles and opens the confectionery box.

Lucas takes a shortbread cookie and tells me he'll call someone to pick up the case of water because he has to stay at his post. I take a few bottles out of the case and thank him. April and I continue walking; he doesn't stop us.

"Megan!" Dina is waving her hand above her head and running toward us. "It's so nice to see a familiar face." She throws herself into my arms.

We sway and I rub circles in her back while Dina squeezes me like a lifebuoy and cries. Meanwhile, April reaches into my tote bag and finds the portable tissue case. When I pull away from Dina, I introduce her to April. I hand Dina a bottle of water, and April offers her a tissue.

Dina leads us to the Muskoka chairs that surround the fire pit beside the cottage. She sniffles and places her hand over mine. The skin around her red, swollen eyes is puffy and blotchy.

"Claire is dead," she says.

"I'm sorry," I respond, not letting on that I already know.

"She was my best friend." Dina breaks into a loud sob as she finishes her sentence.

This isn't what Claire said. I'm sure she said Dina was just her assistant, and they were barely friends. Maybe Claire misled me about their relationship to protect her privacy. When Claire gave me her business card, she said she keeps her professional and private lives separate. And Rick mentioned that privacy was her biggest priority when choosing rental accommodation.

I suppose it's possible Dina's interpretation of their relationship differs from Claire's. Regardless of how close their friendship was, they spent a lot of time together, even staying in the same cottage.

"I'm so happy you're here," Dina says when she composes herself. "Thank you both for coming." She looks at April, then back to me. "How did you get my number?" she asks.

"Claire gave me her card," I explain. "It has contact information for both of you."

She nods. "I'm glad she did."

An officer comes over and asks Dina if he can speak with her. She excuses herself, takes a couple of tissues for the road, and steps away with him.

"I heard you were here!" Eric says, walking toward us. He bends down and kisses the top of my head. "Why are you here?" he rubs my shoulders.

"Dina asked me to come," I reply.

"Why?" he asks, looking confused.

I shrug. "I'm the only person she knows in Harmony Lake, and it's scary to be at a crime scene alone. Also, I brought you a couple of sandwiches since you're working late. They're in my car."

April offers Eric a cookie, and he chooses oatmeal chocolate chip—I knew he would—and I give him a bottle of water. His phone dings.

"Claire's agent is here," he says. "I need to talk to him. I'll see you later."

April gives him the box of cookies and instructs him to share them with his colleagues.

"Oooh, who's the mysterious-looking, handsome guy?" April asks, using her chin to point behind me.

I turn to see who she's referring to.

"Brooks Wiley," I say, watching Eric introduce himself to the well-dressed man. "He's Claire's literary agent." I look at April and smirk. She smirks back. We lean toward each other, meeting halfway. "I saw him making out with Jules Janssen," I whisper.

"Really?" she asks, craning her neck and peering around me to look at him. "I can see it. They're both beautiful."

"I can't stay here tonight," Dina announces, marching back to the fire pit with the officer she was talking to. "Not that I want to stay here, but I don't have anywhere else to go."

I'm about to assure her that April and I will help her find a room at a local hotel, when Brooks comes charging toward us with Eric close behind.

"Dina, what happened?" Brooks demands, then jerks his thumb behind him, toward Eric. "Is he telling the truth? Is Claire dead?"

Brooks's accent is a cross between British and Caribbean. It's beautiful and melodic, like he's speaking in cursive. The accent adds to the intensity of his charisma. I can see why Jules Janssen is attracted to him, but he still makes me anxious. When he's around, his chaotic energy makes me hyper-aware of my surroundings, and a small knot forms in my stomach.

Dina nods, her eyes welling up with tears again. "It's true," she mutters. "I didn't tell you on the phone because I didn't want you to drive here upset."

I stand up so Brooks can have my Muskoka chair. "Dina, if you need me, I'll be under that tree"—I point to a nearby sugar maple—"calling around to find you a room for tonight."

Dina nods and mouths, "Thank you."

"I'll go with you," April declares, standing up. "We can divide and conquer."

Three phone calls later, neither April nor I have any luck finding a room for Dina. The motel and two local resorts are booked because the book fair starts tomorrow. I'm about to call Rick Ransan and ask if he or any of his property-investor friends have somewhere for Dina to stay when she rushes over with Brooks and a uniformed police officer by her side, her blonde hair bobbing as she walks.

"Brooks found a room for me," she declares.

"I'm staying at King of the Hill," he explains in his hypnotic accent. "The manager said he can squeeze her in for one night. But she has to check out by 11 a.m., because they're fully booked for the book fair."

That's a relief, I was considering inviting her to stay at chez Martel.

"Now that you're sorted, April and I should get going," I say. "Dina, if you need anything, call me."

"Can one of you drive me to the hotel?" Dina asks, looking back and forth between me and Brooks. "Claire and I drove here together in her car. It doesn't feel right to drive it now... without her here."

"I can't leave yet. The police need to talk to me," Brooks explains, looking at me.

"I want to get out of here as soon as possible. I'd rather not wait for him," Dina says. "I understand if it's out of your way…"

"It's not out of our way," I interrupt.

"Of course, we'll drive you," April adds.

"Can you wait a few minutes?" Dina asks. She points to the officer standing just behind her. "He's going to escort me inside to pack an overnight bag."

I nod. "We're parked about halfway down the drive-way," I tell her. "We'll meet you in the car."

Dina and the officer turn and head toward the cottage.

Eric walks April and me to the car so he can collect the sandwiches I brought for him.

The officer who accompanied Dina into the cottage walks her to the car. Besides an overnight bag, she has a box of tissues. The drive to King the Hill is quiet. Dina sits in the back seat, crying into a tissue, and I check on her regularly in the rearview mirror.

April and I escort Dina inside the hotel and wait while she checks in. When she has a room number and a cardkey, we walk her to the elevator and hug her goodbye.

"Thank you, Megan." Dina touches my hand. "Thank you, April." She touches April's hand. "I'm so grateful I met you."

For the first time today, Dina smiles.

CHAPTER 7

"Hey, Handsome." I place my needle-felting stuff on the coffee table and turn off the TV. "You're home earlier than I expected."

"I'm home earlier than I expected too," Eric responds, dropping himself onto the sofa next to me. "We've done everything we can for today. The cottage is off the grid. There's no electricity, so we'd have to bring in generators and lights. The propane-fueled lights inside are too dim to work at night. When the sun went down, we called it a day." Sophie jumps onto the sofa and rests her front paws on his lap. Eric rubs her instinctively. She's trained us well.

I cozy up to him and put my head on his chest. "Do you want to talk about it?" I offer, hoping he'll say yes.

"Claire was alone in a locked room. The door was locked from the inside," he discloses.

"Do you know how she died?" I ask.

"It looks like she fell on her needle," he replies.

I cringe and point to my felting needle on the coffee table. "Her felting needle?" I clarify.

I feel him nod.

Felting needles have small barbs that catch the scales of the fibre and force them together. The more you stab, the more solid and felt-like the fibre becomes. The needles are super sharp, and because of the barbs, if you stab yourself, it hurts more than a regular needle. It hurts more when you pull the needle out than it does going in.

"Did she hit an artery or something?" I ask.

"That's the thing," he says. "It didn't look like a fatal wound. But she was alone in the room. There's no other explanation. The door was locked from the inside. We found the key on the desk with her cell phone. Her cell phone was turned off. Something about her death doesn't feel right."

"Uh-oh," I tease, "my intuition is rubbing off on you."

"We found her by the door," he explains. "Her body blocked the door from opening all the way. I think she was trying to escape by picking the lock with the felting needle."

"Why would she pick the lock?" I ask. "The key was in the room with her."

This is the strangest accidental death I've heard of.

"The coroner and I asked the same question," he says. "The coroner thinks Claire could have been confused in her last moments. He's hesitant to declare her death an accident. After we rolled her onto her back and he looked her over, the coroner hinted that the cause of death might not be the puncture wound. He said he'll run a few tests and tell me more tomorrow."

"Did Dina shed any light on what happened?"

Eric shrugs and sighs. "She says Claire went into the den to work. She said it's common for Claire to lock the door and turn off her phone when she's working. According to Dina, Claire likes to work in silence, uninterrupted. Dina says she went down to the lake and sat on the dock. She said she read, then talked to her parents on the phone. She was on the phone with her parents for about an hour. Her cell phone records and her parents' statements verify she's telling the truth.

"Also, there's an excellent view of the dock from the neighbouring cottage. The family staying there said they saw Dina sitting on the dock. Dina says when she returned to the cottage, Claire was still in the den. She says she texted to ask Claire what she wanted for dinner, but Claire didn't answer. Dina assumed Claire's phone was off because she was still working. She waited a while longer, then knocked on the door. When Claire didn't answer, Dina said she panicked and pounded on the door, screaming Claire's name. When Claire still didn't answer, she called Rick. She said she had a feeling Claire was in trouble."

"You've done everything you can do until you hear from the coroner," I assure him.

"We secured the crime scene, and I assigned officers to guard it, just in case."

Crime scene. He called it a crime scene. Subconsciously, Eric believes Claire's death was murder. I hope he's wrong.

CHAPTER 8

FRIDAY, April 16th

"I can't believe Sherlock Holmes is standing in my store," I gush, accepting the maple pecan latte he offers me. "Thank you." The cape makes Eric's broad shoulders appear even broader. If capes ever come back in style, he's all set.

To commemorate the first day of the book fair, attendees, and almost everyone else in town, are dressed up as their favourite literary character.

"Who are you supposed to be?" Sherlock Holmes asks, putting his pretend pipe in his mouth.

"I'm the Paperbag Princess," I say, as if it should be obvious. "You know, from the Robert Munsch book?"

Eric shrugs his caped shoulders. "Never heard of it."

I look at my costume; a paper yard waste bag with holes cut out for my head and arms, and a tiara. It screams Paperbag Princess.

"Seriously?" I'm incredulous. "It was one of Hannah's favourite books when she was little. We read it to her every night at bedtime for at least two years. It's about a princess who uses her wits to save herself and the prince from the fire-breathing dragon."

"Then it's the perfect costume for you," he says, redeeming himself and giving me a kiss that makes the butterflies in my tummy flutter.

"You look pretty handsome, Sherlock."

"Thank you," he says, straightening his deerstalker cap. "What is Sophie supposed to be?" he asks, nodding at the costumed corgi. "Snakes don't have antennae."

"She's not a snake," I say, disappointed. "She's The Very Hungry Caterpillar." Eric shakes his head. "From the Eric Carle book?" I hint.

"Another kids' book?" he assumes.

"A classic in children's literature," I correct him. "I must've read it to Hannah at least a thousand times."

"Have you heard from your dad?" he asks. "What time are you expecting them?"

"We talked this morning," I reply. "He said they'll arrive after lunch."

"Did you tell him about Claire?"

I shake my head. "I decided against it. They still have a two-hour drive ahead of them, and it's best if they aren't emotional."

"Good call," Eric agrees.

"Have you heard from the coroner yet?" I ask.

He shakes his head and puts his magnifying glass—

which I assume is part of his costume—in his pocket. "It's still early. I'm sure he'll be in touch today. I'll be back to welcome your dad and Zoe." He straightens my tiara and kisses me goodbye.

"ARE THEY HERE YET?" The Mad Hatter asks, charging through the front door.

I shake my head. "They're two minutes away," I reply. "They pulled over when they got off the highway and Zoe texted me." After which, I texted everyone else to assemble at Knitorious ASAP.

Adam looks relieved. He slides the pocket watch from his vest pocket and checks the time. He slips the watch back into his pocket and straightens the chain attached to it. "This get-up is warmer than it looks." He takes a handkerchief from his pocket, lifts his velour top hat, and wipes his brow. His dark hair sticks to his forehead.

Adam is a very tall Mad Hatter. The top hat creates the illusion that he's several inches taller than his six feet.

Madame Defarge straightens my ill-fitting head-piece. "Keep your chin up, my dear, or your tiara will slip."

Excellent advice for life in general, not just when I'm wearing a literal tiara.

I smile. "Thank you, Connie."

"Madame Defarge, right?" Eric asks Connie. "The knitter from, A Tale of Two Cities?"

"Well deduced, Sherlock," Connie praises him.

"Elementary," he says with a smile. "See, I read. I just don't read kids' books," he mumbles at me with a wink.

Nancy Drew jumps up from the sofa in the cozy sitting area. "They just pulled into the parking lot!" she announces. "I'll open the back door, so they don't have to walk around to the front."

"Thanks, April!" I say.

On her way to the back door, she puts on her fake glasses, smooths the plaid skirt that matches her plaid hair band, and straightens the sleeves of her cardigan. The cardigan, part of a twinset, is draped over her shoulders with the sleeves tied in front of her chest.

"There's my little bean!" My dad comes toward me with his arms open wide.

"Bean?" Eric mumbles.

"Short for jelly bean," Adam explains to him in hushed tones. "I don't know why."

My dad has an air of distinction about him. It might be the full head of thick silver hair, or the sport jacket-turtleneck combo that has become his trademark uniform, or a combination of both. He's not a tall man. He's only a few inches taller than me, but I swear every time we see each other he's a little shorter than I remember.

"Hi, Dad!" We hug and sway. He kisses my cheek. "How was your drive?" I ask as we pull apart. Looking into his hazel eyes always unnerves me at first, because they're so similar to mine.

"Longer than necessary," Zoe interjects, nudging her husband out of the way and coming in for a hug. "You know your father, Megan. One of his superpowers is taking a short drive and making it long," she jokes.

I wouldn't call the five-hour drive from Toronto to Harmony Lake short, but it's all relative, I guess.

Zoe holds my shoulders and appraises me at arm's length. Her blue eyes inspect me, and her short, blonde curls bob when she nods with approval.

"You look wonderful, Megan," Zoe comments, still looking me up and down. "I suppose we can thank Sherlock for that?"

Blushing, I introduce Eric to Mitchell and Zoe Monroe. Mitchell nods and extends his hand for Eric to shake.

"It's a pleasure to meet you, sir," Eric says, his anxiety palpable.

"Likewise," Mitchell acknowledges before moving along to hug Connie.

"You must call him Mitchell," Zoe says to Eric, engulfing him in a friendly hug. "Calling him 'sir' will go to his head, and that's the last thing we need." She winks and we laugh. "And you'll call me Zoe."

"Nice to meet you, Zoe," Eric says.

Zoe moves on to hug Adam.

Mitchell greets everyone, including Sophie, before he greets Adam. They are cool but cordial to each other.

"Before I forget, Bean, this is for you." Mitchell hands me a thick, letter-size, sealed envelope.

"Thank you, Dad," I say, knowing it's a signed copy of his latest book.

He personally delivers a signed copy of the manuscript for each book he writes to my sister and me. He seals the manuscript in an envelope and signs the seal. My sister and I think it's a personal superstition. I display them in a bookcase. Books aren't small, and Mitchell is a prolific writer, so over the years, we've installed additional bookcases to house them.

"Keep it safe," Mitchell warns with his eyebrows raised.

"I will," I assure him, slipping it under the counter and placing it in my bag.

After everyone greets one another, and I serve refreshments, we sit around the harvest table. When Mitchell and Zoe arrived, Connie locked the door and turned the sign from OPEN to CLOSED. Business would've been dead today, anyway, with the book fair opening, and this isn't a conversation we want to have with customers browsing nearby.

My father marvels at the bookish cookies Tamara made for his Shark Attack book series, and Zoe takes photos of the cookies and of her and Mitchell posing with them.

I'm about to break the news to them about Claire's death. The five of us—me, Eric, April, Connie, and Adam—decided it was best to tell them as soon as they arrived to ensure they didn't hear it from someone else.

Eric says Claire's death will become public knowledge at noon when her family and publisher release a joint statement to the press. It's after 11 a.m., so I'm sure the Harmony Lake rumour mill is on the job, news of her death has somehow leaked, and is already spreading throughout the community.

"Dad," I say, placing my hand on his. He places his other hand on top of mine. "You know they scheduled Claire Rivera to attend the book fair this year, right?"

"I'm aware," he says, sounding agitated. "I noticed when we were driving through town that there are more posters promoting Claire's attendance at the book fair than my attendance. The posters refer to her as the guest of honour. I thought *I* was the guest of honour. There can only be *one* guest of honour, Bean. Is it me or Claire Rivera?"

Here we go. Mitchell doesn't like to share the spotlight. While I'm sure the news of Claire's death will shock and sadden him, I'm worried part of him will resent her death eclipsing his appearance at the event.

"Actually, Dad, I think the posters refer to her as *a* guest of honour." I shake my head and force myself to stay on task. "Regardless, there's been a development regarding Claire's attendance…"

"Oh, I already know about it, Bean." He waves his hand as if it's old news.

"You do?" I ask, squeezing my brows together. "What did you hear?"

Mitchell shrugs. "I heard the same thing as everyone else. Claire Rivera is ending her book series," he says. "I'm not surprised. Writing the same characters book after book isn't for everyone," he justifies. "But her decision to announce it at a book fair we're both attending is uncouth and shows the lengths she'll go to ensure she's the centre of attention."

I inhale deeply. Under the table, Eric gives my knee a reassuring squeeze.

"There's more, Dad," I say as I exhale. "Claire died yesterday."

Zoe gasps and places a hand on her husband's shoulder. "Mitchell, did you hear that?" she whispers.

He nods without breaking eye contact with me. His eyes fill with moisture. "She was too young." His voice catches on the last word. "Are you sure?" His voice is just above a whisper.

I nod. "We're sure. Her family is issuing a statement at noon."

"What happened?" he asks. He looks at Eric. "You're the police chief, what happened?"

"The cause of Claire's death hasn't been released," Eric says in his cop voice.

The lunacy of this situation strikes me. Here we are, seven people sitting around a table, five of us dressed as literary characters, with a corgi under the table dressed as a caterpillar. Having a serious conversation about a tragic death. If it wasn't so sad, it would be laughable.

"Was it an accident?" Mitchell probes. Eric purses his lips into a tight line, then opens his mouth to say something, but Mitchell beats him to it. "It was her nut allergy, wasn't it?"

"Umm... nut allergy?" I ask. "Claire had a nut allergy?" This is the first I've heard of it.

Mitchell gives me an exaggerated nod. "She did," he confirms. "When she worked for me, I would tell her to be more diligent about her allergy before it killed her."

"What do you mean diligent?" Eric asks.

"She was lackadaisical about carrying her EpiPen with her." Mitchell looks at his wife. "Wasn't she, Zoe?"

Zoe nods in agreement. "When Mitchell would attend events, Claire would forget to bring her EpiPen with her. She would work at our house and not have it with her. It made us so nervous that we bought one and kept it handy whenever she was around."

"Did you ever need it?" I ask.

"No," Mitchell and Zoe reply in stereo. "Thank goodness," Zoe adds.

Thinking back, when Claire attended the needle-felting exhibit at the store, she used a napkin to pick up the bookish cookie when I asked her if I could take a picture of her holding it. She didn't partake in any refreshments, avoiding the refreshment table altogether, and hanging out at the front of the store instead. To avoid touching anything, she kept her hands clasped behind her back. Actions that I interpreted as stand-offish might have been part of her safety protocol because of her nut allergy. Things aren't always as they seem.

We're still sitting at the harvest table at noon, albeit in a much more sombre mood, when our phones ding, chime, buzz, and vibrate.

"The statement about Claire's death," Adam advises us, standing up. "I should go. The mayor's office is issuing a statement about Claire's passing, since she died here and was attending our book fair."

Zoe thanks him for coming and gives him a big hug.

"I'll see you out," I say, standing up.

"Thank you for coming," I say at the back door. "I know Mitchell isn't your favourite person. I appreciate you putting aside your feelings."

Adam shrugs. "You and I are still family, Meg, there-fore Mitchell is still my family, whether he likes it or not." He smirks and puts on his top hat. "I'll see you tomorrow at dinner."

I lock the door behind him and turn around. "Jeez!" I say, clutching my chest. "You scared the life out of me." Eric is standing partway up the stairs that lead to his apartment. How is this tall, muscular man so light on his feet?

"Sorry, babe," Eric says, chuckling. "I'll be upstairs talking to the coroner." He holds up the phone in his hand, then disappears upstairs.

I hope it's good news, if there is such a thing when someone dies young and unexpectedly. Good news would be if the coroner determines natural causes or a freak accident caused Claire's death. The anxious knot in my stomach isn't expecting good news.

CHAPTER 9

ONLY IN HARMONY Lake can the Paperbag Princess and Nancy Drew walk The Very Hungry Caterpillar on a leash, through the park, with no sideways glances or second looks.

"Do you think I should have taken off Sophie's costume?" I ask.

"She's fine," April says. "She doesn't even notice it."

"You're right." I nod in agreement. "Now reassure me that Claire didn't eat a nut product at Knitorious on Wednesday afternoon, then die from it twenty-four hours later."

"It's not possible, Megabean," April reassures me, mashing up her nickname for me with my father's nickname for me. "Besides, nothing had nuts in it. T made sure the bookish cookies were nut free. I helped you put the food out, you served nothing with nuts. Anyway, nut allergies kill in like thirty minutes or something." She stops walking and looks at me. "Did Eric tell you Claire died because of her nut allergy?"

I shake my head. "No," I reply. "He doesn't know her cause of death. He's talking to the coroner right now, though, so he'll know soon."

When we get to Artsy Tartsy, April and I hug good-bye, and I watch her cross the street and go inside the bakery. Then Sophie and I turn around and meander toward Knitorious. It's a beautiful spring day. The sun is shining, and the birds are singing. The temperature is a mild ten degrees—maybe a tad cooler this close to the lake.

Connie accompanied Mitchell and Zoe to chez Martel to help them settle in. I offered to go with them, but they said they have a lot to catch up on, and I didn't want to be in the way.

I closed Knitorious for the rest of the day since nobody is shopping today with the opening ceremony for the book fair and the news of Claire's death.

"Come here, Soph. Let's take off your costume." I crouch down to her level and undo the clasps that keep Sophie's costume in place, then pull it off. She gives herself a good shake. "Is that better?" I ask, scratching her neck and chest. "Who's a good girl?"

I give her a few dog treats, then take off my paper leaf bag and lay it over the back of one of the kitchenette chairs. I'm about to make lunch, and cooking in a paper dress isn't how I want to die. I take the glass container of stuffed peppers out of the fridge and climb the stairs to Eric's apartment.

"Shhh," I remind Sophie. "He might be on the phone." I open the door and Sophie rushes in ahead of me.

She jumps onto the leather sofa and parks herself next to Eric, who's leaning forward, focused on the laptop on the coffee table in front of him. His Sherlock Holmes costume lays over the back of the leather club chair. His phone is on the table next to his laptop, and there are no AirPods in his ears.

"Hey, Handsome," I say.

"Hey, babe!" He looks up at me and smiles. He's not on the phone. "No more Paperbag Princess?" he asks.

"Not until after lunch," I reply. "Hungry?" I ask, holding up the glass container.

"Starving," he responds. "What are we having?"

He's always starving. I've never seen Eric turn down a meal.

"Stuffed peppers," I reply. "The ones you like with the sausage, rice, and cheesy mushroom stuffing. How hungry are you?"

Still absorbed in whatever is on the computer screen, he holds up two fingers; he's two peppers hungry. I put the peppers in the oven and join him on the sofa. "Anything interesting?" I ask.

He sighs and turns the laptop so I can see the screen. "Crime scene photos," he explains. "From Claire and Dina's cottage."

Crime scene. He said crime scene, not death scene.

"The coroner concluded Claire was murdered?" I ask, flexing my deductive muscle.

"Fatal anaphylaxis," he replies, nodding. "I need to find the source of the peanut oil and retrace Claire's final steps to explain how she came into contact with it. It could be accidental, but it's too suspicious. Too many things don't add up."

I take a deep breath and let it out. "So, it was her peanut allergy that killed her, not the felting needle?"

He nods again. "The coroner believes she fell on the felting needle when she collapsed. The puncture wound from the needle was not fatal."

"Why was she hanging out near the door with her felting needle?" I wonder aloud. "I mean, she probably realized she was in trouble. Why didn't she use the key? Or use her cell phone to call for help?"

The rental cottage—like the rest of Harmony Lake— is remote, but we have decent cell phone coverage. Unlike some remote towns, we lucked out with cell phone towers.

"The coroner says the allergic reaction could have made Claire confused, panicky, or both. Maybe she couldn't immediately find the key or her phone, but she found the felting needle. Or maybe she was already holding it when the reaction started."

I nod toward the laptop screen. "Are you searching the crime scene photos for the nut product she had contact with?" I ask.

He nods and sighs. "Officers are searching the cottage for anything that might contain nuts. So far, nothing, but they've collected a bunch of stuff for the lab to test."

"Is that the letter Jules asked me to give to Claire?" I ask, pointing at the handwritten note on the screen.

Eric nods. "I assume it is. It's signed by Jules." He reaches for the laptop and zooms in on the photo. "Is that the envelope she gave you?"

"Yes," I confirm. "I remember her pretty, cursive handwriting."

The oven beeps, and I plate the stuffed peppers. Eric closes his laptop and joins me at the breakfast bar.

"Did your dad say anything after I left?" he asks.

I blow on a forkful of steaming hot stuffing before I reply. "He said lots of things," I tease. "Are you asking if he said anything about you?"

"I can't get a read on him. I don't think he likes me, but I can't tell for sure."

I shrug. "That's how he is," I explain. "You can't spend your life worrying about whether my dad likes you." I smile. "I already know how I feel about you, and his opinion won't change my mind."

"He posted a nice statement about Claire," Eric says, then takes a sip of water.

"Zoe or his publisher posted a nice statement," I correct him.

When Zoe and my dad met, she was an editor with the publishing company that handles his books. She still edits for him, but since Claire quit as his assistant ten years ago, Zoe stepped into that role too.

"Your dad lets other people post to his social media accounts?"

"*Only* other people post to my dad's social media accounts," I clarify. "I don't think Mitchell Monroe has ever made a social media post. I bet he doesn't even know how to access his accounts." We laugh. "I didn't know you follow my dad on social media."

"I don't," Eric explains, "but I'm monitoring the responses to Claire's death, and the responses to yesterday's post about retiring the Familia series."

I gasp. "You think an angry fan killed her because she was ending the series?"

"It's possible," he acknowledges. "Babe, there were some disturbing, threatening social media posts after her announcement."

"Ugh!" I roll my eyes. "Social media can be so negative and toxic."

"Interpol contacted me about one post in particular," he discloses.

"Interpol? The international police organization?" I ask.

After eating half of my pepper, I'm full. I use my fork to push the other half to the edge of the plate. Eric scoops up my abandoned pepper with his fork and transfers it to his plate. Where does he put all the food he eats? It's one of the great mysteries of the world; he eats enough for three people, yet there isn't an ounce of fat on him. I'm jealous.

He nods. "Claire has an overzealous fan from Britain who made some particularly vitriolic comments and vague threats yesterday when Claire announced the end of *Familia*. Authorities in Britain tried to question her, but she's abroad."

"Well, if she's not in Harmony Lake, she can't be a suspect in Claire's murder," I surmise.

"That's the thing," he says. "We think she's in Harmony Lake. She landed in Toronto a few days ago and rented a car at the airport. Her cell phone has been dinging off local cell phone towers. I'm waiting for the car rental company to call me back. I'm hoping the rental car she's using has GPS, and they can tell me where it is. I'd like to talk to her."

"Did you check the local hotels?" I ask.

He nods as he finishes his second pepper and digs into my abandoned half-pepper. "She hasn't checked in anywhere."

I bite the inside of my cheek. "Maybe she's renting one of the rental properties. I can ask around. What's her name?"

"Piper Peters," Eric replies, standing up and retrieving his phone from the coffee table. "I'll send you her picture. If you see her, let me know."

"Of course," I say, looking at my phone when it dings. Piper Peters is about my age. In this photo, her long, straight brown hair is in a low ponytail that hangs over her shoulder. She has deep-set brown eyes and fair skin. Her nose and mouth are small, and her lips are pursed in a tight line. "Is this a mugshot?" I ask.

"I think so," Eric responds. "She has a history of harassment and threatening. Brooks Wiley mentioned Piper yesterday when I asked him who might want to harm Claire. He said Claire got a restraining order against her last year when Piper showed up on her doorstep and demanded that she change the end of one of the *Familia* books."

"That doesn't sound like the behaviour of a mentally well person," I observe.

"It isn't," Eric agrees. "So, if you see her, please, please, don't approach her. Call me."

I nod.

"Promise?" he asks.

"Promise."

CHAPTER 10

"HI, DAD." We kiss cheeks.

He's sitting in one of the living room chairs. His reading glasses are on the tip of his nose, and he's reading on his iPad.

"How are you, Bean?" he asks, looking at me over his glasses and smiling.

"Fine," I reply. "Where are Zoe and Connie?"

Mitchell closes his iPad and places it on the table next to him. He pats his lap, and Sophie jumps onto it.

"They went to the town square to revel in the book fair festivities," he replies, scratching Sophie between the ears.

"Maybe I'll join them," I suggest.

"They shouldn't be hard to find." He sounds amused. "Just look for Madame Defarge and Charlotte." He chuckles.

"Charlotte?" I ask.

"Yes, Charlotte," he reiterates. "Zoe dressed as Charlotte, the spider from Charlotte's Web."

"You didn't put on a costume and join them?" I smirk at the mental image of Mitchell Monroe dressed up as anything.

"It's not my scene," says the author about the book fair.

"Right," I say. "There's a strawberry dream cake in the fridge. Tamara made it just for you."

"I found it," he says, as if it's a secret. "And if Zoe asks, *you* had an enormous slice." He raises his index finger to his lips in a *shhh* motion. "I'm supposed to be watching my sugar intake."

"Got it," I say with a dramatic wink. "So how are you feeling?"

"Do you mean after the enormous slice of cake, or about Claire's untimely death?" he answers my question with a question.

"I know you weren't on good terms and hadn't spoken in ten years, but it must be a shock."

Mitchell sighs. "It is," he admits. "Regardless of our feelings toward one another, Claire was too young to die. She had her entire life to look forward to. I'm debating reaching out to her family. Zoe said we should send flowers and a note."

"That's a lovely idea," I concur. "Phillip can make you a floral arrangement."

I remind him that my neighbour at home and at work, Phillip, owns a florist shop. I'm about to tell my dad about the coroner determining Claire's death was murder, but my phone rings. It's Dina Langley.

"Excuse me, Dad."

He waves me away and puts his head back, closing his eyes. He's still rubbing Sophie, who has fallen asleep in his lap.

"Hello?" I answer the call on the way to my bedroom.

"Hi, Megan! It's Dina."

"Hi, Dina. I've been thinking about you. I meant to text you, but I haven't had a spare moment."

"That's OK. I understand. Thank you again for stopping your life to come to the cottage yesterday. I appreciate it."

"No problem," I say.

Claire's death being declared a murder hangs between us like a dense fog.

"I have to collect the rest of my things from the cottage," Dina says. "There was a cancellation and the hotel manager said I can stay here. Since the cottage is a crime scene, I can't stay there, anyway." I hear her gasp. "Not that I'd want to stay there," she corrects herself. "I feel safer at the hotel. They have cameras here, and it's booked solid, so if something happens, someone will hear me scream." Another gasp. "That sounds awful. I'm not very articulate today. I didn't sleep well and…"

"It's OK, Dina," I interrupt her. "You don't have to

explain. I get it. I can come with you if it would help. I closed the store for the rest of the day anyway…"

"Thank you, Megan! It would be easier if I'm not alone. I mean, I could ask Brooks to go with me, but he's not very warm and comforting, you know? He's all business, all the time. And I think Claire's… death created more work for him."

He didn't look all business, all the time when I saw him kissing Jules Janssen and touching her butt. Just saying.

"Should I pick you up?" I offer.

"No, thank you," Dina replies. "I arranged a rental car, and Brooks drove me to pick it up this morning. I'm more emotionally stable than I was yesterday… well, somewhat… I'll drive myself."

We agree on a time to meet at the cottage and end our call.

"Dad, I have to go out. Do you need anything?" I call as I enter the living room. "Dad?" Where did he go?

"No, Bean. I'm fine." He's at the front door, putting on his shoes. "I think I'll take a walk and burn off the cake I ate, so I can eat more later." He winks.

"You mean you'll burn off the cake *I* ate." I wink back.

"That's my girl." He chuckles. "I'll take my granddog with me, and we can explore the neighbourhood." He refers to Sophie as his granddog.

"Take your cell phone, in case you need it," I remind him.

"Yes, Bean. Stop worrying. You get that from your mother."

We kiss cheeks. He attaches Sophie's leash, and they leave.

THERE ARE as many vehicles along the narrow, winding driveway as there were yesterday. Also like yesterday, I find a spot between two cars about halfway up, parallel park, and walk the rest of the way. I don't know if Dina is here yet because I don't know what kind of rental car she's driving.

I hear Lucas's voice before I see him. Lucas Butler is the rookie officer who was standing guard at the top of the driveway yesterday, the one who has a crush on my daughter.

"I'm sorry, sir, but you're not on the list. If you're not on the list, you can't pass."

"Of course, I'm on the list!" I recognize that dulcet accent. Brooks Wiley is here, and it sounds like Lucas won't let him access the crime scene. "I insist you let me pass, or I will call Chief Sloane, and he will have your badge!"

"Hi, Lucas," I say, approaching the two men.

"Hi, Megan!" Lucas smiles. "No water or cookies today?" he teases.

"Not today," I reply. "Is Dina Langley here?" Lucas purses his lips and shrugs. "Long blonde hair.

Young"—well, young to me. I forgot I'm talking about a twenty-three-year-old—"she left with April and me yesterday."

Recognition flashes across his face. "Right!" he declares. "I remember her." He shakes his head. "I haven't seen her."

"I'm supposed to meet her here. Is it OK if I wait in the Muskoka chairs by the fire pit?" I ask, pointing toward the cottage.

"Of course," Lucas replies. "I'll tell her where you are when she shows up."

I thank him, smile at both men, and continue walking.

"So, you're telling me she's on the list and I'm not?" Brooks says, seething with frustration. "I need to get in that house. You don't understand. There's money at stake."

This gets my attention, and I stop walking.

"If you aren't on the list, you don't get in."

Lucas and Brooks continue arguing back and forth, Brooks holding up his phone, threatening to call Eric, and Lucas telling him to call whoever he wants. They're at an impasse. I'm about to continue on my way to the firepit when I hear Dina's high-pitched, excited voice.

"Call the police!" she yells. "Call the police!"

She's yelling this at a police officer. There are literally half a dozen cops here.

I jog down the driveway until she's in view. She's

flailing her arms and running up the steep driveway like she's being chased.

"Brooks! It's her! She's here! Call the police," Dina yells when she spots Brooks. "She's crazy! She says Claire isn't dead!"

Who says Claire isn't dead?

Lucas puts his hand on his sidearm and positions himself in front of Brooks. With his other hand, he beckons Dina, encouraging her to keep running toward him.

"Who is Dina talking about?" I ask, running toward Lucas and Brooks.

"I don't have a clue." Brooks looks confused.

He mumbles something I can't hear as he jogs toward her. Then he turns and, wide-eyed, runs back toward Lucas and cowers behind him. "That woman is crazy! Arrest her before she hurts someone!"

What woman is crazy? Is he talking about Dina?

Then I hear her shrieking British accent.

"I demand to know what's happening! Where is Claire Rivera! Who is in charge?"

Piper Peters. I recognize her from the photo Eric showed me earlier.

I move to the edge of the driveway and crouch between two parked cars. I've already dialed Eric's number.

"Hello?" He's in the car. I can tell from the echo.

"Piper Peters is here," I hiss.

"Where are you?"

"Rental cottage," I whisper, trying to talk to him and listen to Piper's ravings.

"Why are you at the cottage? Never mind. Are you sure it's her?"

"Positive."

"Don't approach her," he reminds me.

CHAPTER 11

WE END our call and three officers run down the driveway from the cottage. They apprehend Piper without incident. I emerge from my hiding spot and join Brooks and Dina.

"The chief says to take her to the station for questioning. He'll meet you there," Lucas tells the officer who's placing Piper in his patrol car.

Piper looks at the three of us—me, Dina, and Brooks—from the backseat. Her face is taut, and her lips pressed into a taut line. She and I lock eyes until the patrol car drives away and forces us to break eye contact. There are so many questions I want to ask her.

Lucas clears up the confusion about Brooks being on the list and gives all three of us–me, Dina, and Brooks– permission to pass. The officer who accompanies us searches our bags and pockets to ensure we don't have anything that might contaminate the crime scene, then we proceed to the cottage.

It's large and modern. The entire back wall is floor-to-ceiling windows and French doors with a beautiful view of the lake. The space is open and airy, with simple, contemporary furnishings. With four bedrooms, it's large for only two people, but I understand why Claire and Dina chose this specific cottage in this precise location. It's tidy, clean, and private with a beautiful view.

The officer follows Dina into her bedroom, where she lobs an open suitcase onto the queen-sized bed. She tosses clothes and personal effects into the suitcase, packing as if her goal is to get out of here as soon as possible and organize her belongings later. I don't blame her. If my employer-slash-friend met a violent end here, I'd be in a hurry to leave too.

"How can I help?" I ask.

Dina stops tossing items into the suitcase and looks at me. "I left my swimsuit and towel on the clothesline by the dock. And my rubber shoes too."

I nod. "I'll get them," I tell her.

Brooks follows me down to the dock.

"Hi," he says, extending his hand. "I'm Brooks Wiley. I'm–I was–Claire Rivera's agent."

I shake his warm hand. His grip is firm and confident. "Hi, Brooks. I'm Megan Martel. I'm sorry for your loss."

"Oh!" A glint of realization shines in his eyes. "You're Mitchell Monroe's daughter."

"That's right," I affirm.

Did Jules tell him who my father is?

Brooks reaches into the pocket of his light grey, custom-tailored suit and pulls out a business card. "Do you know if your dad is happy with his current literary agent?"

I shrug. "I assume so, he hasn't said otherwise."

He pulls out another business card and hands it to me. "Just in case he's looking to make a change, please give him my card."

Dina wasn't joking when she said Brooks is all business, all the time. I understand Claire's death creates a gap in Brooks's client list, but it seems insensitive to replace her the day after her murder, at the scene of the crime.

"I'll pass it on." I drop the cards in my bag, then remove the towel from the line and fold it. "It's nice of you to help Dina pack her things. Claire's death really shook her up." I hand him the folded towel and pull the swimsuit off the line.

"If Dina is shaken up about anything, she's shaken up about losing her job," Brooks remarks with a contemptuous sneer. "That's what she and Claire were arguing about yesterday before Claire died. Dina was angry because their contract ends the day they release the last *Familia* book."

"Claire and Dina were arguing yesterday before

Claire died?" I confirm. "How do you know?" I hand him the folded swimsuit, and he places it on top of the folded towel I gave him a minute ago.

"I rushed over here as soon as I saw Claire's post about retiring the Familia series," Brooks explains. "I heard them yelling from the driveway. Also, Claire told me once that the contract between them specifies that Dina's role as Claire's assistant ends when the Familia book series ends."

"It sounds like a unique arrangement," I say, gathering magazines and books from a nearby lounge chair. "Claire didn't tell you ahead of time that she was planning to stop writing *Familia*?" I ask.

He shakes his head. "I found out when I saw her social media post, just like everyone else. Dina seemed just as surprised as I was, so I don't think Claire warned her either."

If this is true, was Dina angry enough about losing her job to kill her employer? If Claire's death delays the release of the final *Familia* book, would it also delay Dina's last day on the job? Could Claire's untimely death delay Dina's unemployment status? I wonder if Dina told the police about her argument with Claire?

Claire is one of the world's most successful authors; she's likely Brooks's most successful client and his biggest source of income. Was he so shocked and angry by Claire's announcement that he killed her?

"I was kind of hoping her announcement was a publicity stunt or something."

"It wasn't," Brooks insists. "She was dead serious."

He doesn't seem to realize his unfortunate choice of words.

I add the pile of magazines and books to the towel and swimsuit in Brooks's arms.

"Their entire relationship was unique," he agrees. "They were very secretive, and Claire relied on Dina for almost everything. It was like she couldn't write without her. It doesn't matter what I asked her, Claire always had to check with Dina before she could answer me."

"She sounds like an excellent assistant," I point out. "My dad says an author assistant's job is to make sure the author has nothing to do except write. He says a good assistant takes care of all the menial tasks that writers use to distract themselves from writing." I pick up the rubber shoes, and we head back toward the cottage.

"Using your father's criteria, Dina is a fabulous assistant." Brooks chuckles.

"How did Claire and Dina meet?" I ask.

"I don't know," Brooks admits. "Dina was already her assistant when Claire and I met."

As we approach the back door, I realize this is my last chance to talk to Brooks without being overheard by either Dina or the officer chaperoning us. I stop walking. Brooks stops walking too and looks at me.

"What did you mean when you told the officer money is at stake?" I ask.

"The signed books," Brooks explains. "The ones in the cottage. They were to be sold at Claire's book signing this weekend. They're worth a lot more money today than they were yesterday. Now that Claire has died and can't sign any more books, those signed books will be a hot commodity among her fans and collectors."

"OK," I acknowledge. "Why are they at stake?"

"They can't stay here, Megan," he says, like I'm missing the point. "This cottage has no security. It's secluded and in the middle of nowhere. Do you know how easy it would be to sneak in and steal them?"

"The police are guarding the cottage and its contents," I remind him.

"Not good enough," Brooks counters. "Someone could drive up to the dock in a boat. Or they could sneak through the trees from another cottage." He shakes his head.

It sounds like Brooks Wiley has thought about how to get in and out of the cottage unnoticed.

"I'm supposed to remove them from the cottage and take them somewhere secure. The publishing company asked me to keep them safe until a courier picks them up on Monday," he adds.

We enter the cottage and find Dina in the washroom, stuffing toiletries into an overnight bag. I hold up the rubber shoes, and she puts them in the tote bag. As she takes them, I notice another bandage on one of her fingers.

"Another paper cut?" I ask, nodding to the bandage.

"This?" Dina asks, appraising her injured middle finger. "No. I bite my nails when I'm stressed." She fans out her hand and examines her short nails. "The last twenty-four hours have been extra stressful. I bit this one too low, and it bled."

Brooks extends his arms, showing Dina the towel, swimsuit, and reading material we collected from the dock.

"The magazines aren't ours," Dina explains, pointing to the magazines in Brooks's arms. "They were here when we arrived at the cottage. I took them down to the dock yesterday and forgot to bring them back."

Instead of moving them herself, Dina points to the edge of the tub while looking at the magazines, word-lessly instructing Brooks to place them there. Brooks complies and places the magazines on the tub, then Dina takes the remaining pile of stuff from him and drops it into her overnight bag.

"Good thing it didn't rain," I comment to break up the weird atmosphere between them.

"There," she declares, looking around the wash-room. "I think that's everything."

"Dina, where are the books?" Brooks asks her.

"I figured that's why you're here," Dina replies with a slight huff. "Where will you take them?"

We follow her to the living room, where she points to the boxes of books stacked against a wall. Brooks and Dina discuss possible new locations for the boxes of books. They agree their hotel rooms would be too obvious to anyone hoping to get their hands on them.

Brooks excuses himself to call the hotel to ask if they have a safe or locked room that can accommodate the books.

"I'll ask Eric if there's anything the police can do to help store the books," I suggest, trying to help.

"Eric?" Dina asks.

"Chief Sloane," I clarify as I text him.

"You two are a couple?" she asks.

"Uh-huh,"

"I knew it," she gushes. "I could tell when you were here yesterday. He kept touching you and walked you to your car."

"The books can't stay in the evidence lock-up because they aren't evidence," I say, changing the subject.

"The hotel doesn't have anywhere large enough to store them," Brooks announces upon his return.

"I might have space at Knitorious," I suggest. "I could lock them in the storeroom. They'd blend in with my father's books. The police chief lives in the upstairs apartment, so it's pretty safe."

"That would be perfect!" Brooks says.

"They'd be safe there," Dina adds.

"It will only be until Monday when the courier picks them up," Brooks reminds me.

With that settled, Brooks, Dina, me, and a few officers lug the boxes of books to my and Dina's cars. An officer checks our bags and pockets to ensure we don't leave with anything not on the list of items approved for removal. As much as Brooks insists he'd love to follow us to the store and help us unload the boxes, he has an important meeting and has to rush back to his hotel. How convenient for him.

CHAPTER 12

I PARK AS close as possible to the back door at Knitorious and prop open the door with a brick. One by one, Dina and I unload the boxes of books.

"What are you doing, my dear?" Connie asks.

I explain about transferring Claire's signed books from the cottage to the store for safekeeping.

"What are you doing here?" I ask.

"We parked here and walked to the book fair," Connie explains, gesturing to Zoe who is wearing a black spider costume. "It's a lovely day for a walk. Besides, parking at the venue is a hassle."

I nod.

"Megan, wouldn't it make more sense to take the books to chez Martel?" Zoe asks, all four of her right-side spider legs moving in unison when she gestures with her right hand. "You have that newfangled security system there."

She's right. I nod, then look at Dina and realize she hasn't met my stepmother.

"Dina Langley, this is my stepmum, Zoe Monroe." I gesture to my spider-costumed stepmum. "Zoe, this is Dina Langley, she was Claire Rivera's assistant." I gesture to Dina.

Zoe extends four arms, and after a moment of confusion while she determines which arm is real, Dina shakes Zoe's hand.

Connie and Zoe offer Dina their condolences. Then, after a brief conversation about how much we all love Charlotte's Web, I explain to Dina that my house has a state-of-the-art security system complete with cameras, motion sensors, and police monitoring.

I don't bore her with the details about why I have such an elaborate security system, but the short story is someone broke into the house, lay in wait for me, then tried to kill me. As a result, Adam had the house outfitted with a fancy security system to keep Hannah and me safe.

"I think the boxes would fit in the laundry room," I say.

"That sounds like a better idea," Dina agrees. "I'll call Brooks and make sure he's OK with it." Dina calls Brooks while I return the few boxes we've unloaded to my car. "He's not answering," she says, sliding her phone in her pocket.

"Moving the books without telling him feels sneaky," I say.

"It'll be fine," Dina reassures me. "I'll text him later and explain where we moved them and why."

Dina, Connie, and Zoe all insist it will be fine, and storing the books at chez Martel is a better idea, so I agree and Dina follows me home in her car.

"HEY, BABE." Eric kisses me hello. "Where are Mitchell and Zoe?"

"They went into town to send flowers to Claire's family," I reply.

"Did Sophie go with them?" he asks, looking around his feet where the corgi always rushes to greet him.

I nod. "This is her fifth walk today." I exaggerate with a chuckle. "She loves it when her grandparents visit. We didn't expect you for dinner with the case and all."

"I don't want to miss dinner with your dad and Zoe," he explains. "I can go back to work later." He jerks his thumb toward the laundry room. "What's with the boxes?"

I explain how offering to store Claire's signed books at Knitorious morphed into storing them here. "I wish you'd shown up an hour ago," I tease. "We could have used your muscle to help carry them into the house."

"Brooks Wiley didn't help you?" Eric asks. "He's the person appointed by the publisher to look after them."

"Brooks rushed off to a meeting," I explain, drizzling olive oil onto the baking sheet of baguette pieces.

"What's for dinner?" Eric asks, rubbing his flat stomach. "I'm starving." He's always starving.

"Pesto chicken with roasted zucchini and red pepper panzanella salad," I reply.

"Can I help?"

I decline his offer, then add, "There are pita chips in the cupboard and hummus in the fridge to tide you over until it's ready. How's the case?" I ask.

"I questioned Piper Peters and released her," he replies as he sits at the table and digs into the hummus and pita chips.

"You released her?" I ask, sliding the baking sheet of seasoned bread into the oven. "She's not a suspect?"

"She has an alibi," Eric explains. "It's weak, but it's an alibi. I didn't have enough to keep her. It took a while to make Piper believe Claire is dead. She'd convinced herself it was some kind of elaborate media hoax."

"Denial can be strong," I say. "If Piper killed Claire, she wouldn't be in denial about her death, right?"

Eric shrugs and swallows a mouthful of hummus. "I've seen weirder things."

"Have you heard anything about Dina and Claire having a loud argument yesterday?" I ask, joining him at the table with a cutting board and knife to slice the red peppers and zucchini.

He shakes his head. "No, but it sounds like you have."

I tell Eric that Brooks claimed to hear Claire and Dina's argument from the driveway. Then I tell him about Brooks's revelation that Claire didn't warn anyone she intended to stop writing *Familia*, and Dina's job ends with the book series.

"I bet they were both angry with Claire," Eric theorizes, putting the lid on the hummus container.

"Angry enough to kill her?" I wonder out loud.

"We can't verify Brooks Wiley's alibi," he discloses as he seals the bag of pita chips. "We know he was at the cottage the morning before Claire died. He says he arrived at the hotel and was in his room working on his laptop until hours later when Dina called to tell him Claire died."

"No one saw him come in?" I ask.

"There is video footage of him entering the hotel, and one employee thinks he remembers Brooks entering the hotel, but isn't sure about the time," Eric explains. "Brooks didn't use his keycard. He didn't enter his room. He hasn't used his keycard since he left to go to the cottage yesterday morning. The main entrance is the only door with video surveillance. He could've come and gone through a different door."

"I see," I say, smirking.

"You know something," Eric accuses.

"I suspect something."

"I'm listening," he urges.

"Did anyone access Jules Janssen's room at the time Brooks claims he entered his room?" I ask.

I tell Eric about the intimate moment Brooks and Jules shared in the alley beside my store. "It definitely wasn't the first time they met," I say in conclusion.

Eric types a text to someone, instructing them to ask the hotel for the access history to Jules Janssen's suite of rooms. Then I remember the second time I saw Brooks Wiley.

"He was across the street when Claire and Dina were at Knitorious," I recount. "Dina told me who he was, so I assumed he was waiting for her and Claire." I put down the knife and look at Eric. "In hindsight, I wonder if Jules sent him," I theorize. "Maybe he was watching for Claire to leave with the gift bag from Jules. Maybe Jules dispatched him to report back to her."

"You think Brooks might be a double agent?" Eric asks, grinning with amusement at his pun. "You think he worked for both Claire Rivera and Jules Janssen?"

I shrug and carry the chopped veggies to the counter near the oven. "Maybe," I respond. "You always say motive comes down to either love, money, or ego," I say, removing the toasted bread from the oven and transferring the bread pieces to a bowl. "Think about it. Brooks would earn a lot of money if Jules convinced Claire to turn the *Familia* books into a movie. His fifteen-percent cut would be substantial. And from where I was standing, he looked smitten with Jules. Brooks has at least two motives to kill Claire, money and love." I add the chopped peppers and zucchini to the baking sheet the bread was on and slide it back into the oven.

"Claire can't agree to a *Familia* movie if she's dead," Eric counters.

"No, but her estate can," I remind him as I rub pesto into the chicken breasts. "Maybe Brooks thinks it'll be easier to convince her heirs than to convince Claire herself."

If Brooks killed Claire Rivera, did he act alone, or did he and Jules kill her together?

Sophie charges down the hall, followed by the thud of the front door closing.

"Hey, Soph." She stops long enough for Eric and me to greet her before continuing to her water bowl.

"Can you set the table, please?" I ask Eric while I brown the chicken.

AFTER DINNER, Zoe and my dad yawn and stretch, their eyes heavy with fatigue. It's only early evening, and so far today, they've had a long drive, learned about Claire's death, then learned her death was murder. Zoe walked around town, checking out the book fair dressed as a spider. My dad ate too much cake, and between them, they've put about fifteen miles on Sophie's odometer. They've had a long day, so I insist they relax and let Eric and me clean the kitchen. While

Sophie and her grandparents sink into the sofa and watch the evening news with the volume turned up extra loud, we clear the table, load the dishwasher, and tend to the myriad of other tasks required to make the kitchen look like dinner never happened.

"I'll get this, and you can check in at work," I say, taking the broom from Eric and sweeping crumbs toward the hidden sweep inlet under the kitchen cabinet.

Eric turns on his phone and waits for it to come to life. He makes a point of turning it off every day for at least an hour—a gesture I appreciate—but I know when he's working a big case, it stresses him out to be unreachable.

He reads and replies to texts and emails while his phone dings, rings, buzzes, and vibrates.

"What's wrong?" I stop wiping the stovetop and look at him when he utters a curse word under his breath.

"I don't know how to tell you this, babe." He takes a deep breath. "Your dad is a suspect. I have to question him."

"What?!" I hiss, putting away the broom.

I peek in the family room. My dad is asleep with his head resting on the back of the sofa, and Zoe is asleep with her head on my dad's shoulder. Sophie is asleep, sprawled across their laps. I have to imagine their chorus of gentle snores because I can't hear anything other than the meteorologist on the twenty-four-hour news channel. Thank goodness, they watch the news with the volume so loud and can't overhear our conversation.

"Is this because he knew about Claire's nut allergy and made that stupid comment about how he thought her carelessness about it might kill her?" I struggle to contain myself to a whisper.

Eric shakes his head and opens his mouth to answer me, then closes it, and gestures for me to follow him. We tiptoe to the bedroom where I close the door while he turns on the TV and increases the volume.

"My dad couldn't have killed Claire. He and Zoe were two hours south of here when she died. They pulled off the highway for the night, remember?"

"After they checked in, your dad left the hotel alone. For several hours," Eric explains. "The hotel has surveillance footage."

"OK." I shrug. "That doesn't mean he drove to Harmony Lake and murdered Claire," I claim.

"The problem is, I don't know where he went." Eric throws up his hands in frustration. "The man turns off his cell phone when he's in the car. Who does that?" He sounds flustered. "If I could track his cell phone location, this wouldn't be necessary."

"Why were you looking into him, anyway?" I ask, my voice full of agitation and my cheeks hot.

"I have to eliminate him as a suspect. He was close enough in proximity that it's within the realm of possibility. And because of Mitchell and Claire's troubled history, his name is being bantered around social media as a likely suspect." Eric places his hands on my shoulders. "You might want to avoid reading the social media comments. Some of them are pretty harsh."

I sigh and sit on the edge of the bed. "My dad isn't a murderer." I shake my head and blink away the tears that sting my eyes.

"I know, babe." Eric sits down next to me. "But you know how this works. I have to eliminate him so when we arrest the actual killer, they can't suggest Mitchell as an alternate suspect to create reasonable doubt." He turns his body toward me. "Look at it this way, when I eliminate Mitchell as a suspect, no one can accuse him of killing Claire. I'll make sure his name and reputation are clear."

"Do you have to question Zoe too?" I sigh again.

Eric nods. "I won't take them to the station," he offers. "I can question them myself, so no one else has to know, and it won't leak to the media. I can question them here if they agree."

"My dad might lawyer up," I warn him. "He won't make it easy for you."

Eric shrugs one shoulder. "That's his choice. If it happens, we'll deal with it."

"Not tonight, please?" I implore. "You saw how tired they are. They're sound asleep on the sofa. Can we talk to them about this in the morning?"

Eric nods. "It'll give me more time to work up the

nerve." He looks at me. "Your dad barely tolerates me already. He'll hate me after this."

If it proves he didn't murder Claire, it will be worth it.

Where was my dad when Claire was killed? Why did he leave the hotel after they checked in? Why was he gone for several hours? Does Zoe know where my dad was, and what he was doing?

Speaking of Zoe, what was she doing while Mitchell was unaccounted for? If they weren't together, does she have an alibi? Don't be silly, Megan. Zoe doesn't have a vindictive bone in her body. There's no way she'd kill Claire Rivera out of revenge for stealing her husband's idea. Would she?

CHAPTER 13

Saturday, April 17th

"Good morning, Bean!"

I almost jump out of my skin at the sound of the unexpected voice.

"Good morning, Dad," I say, clutching my chest.

I'm used to being the first person awake in my house. It freaks me out to have another morning person here. Eric is a morning person, but he doesn't hang around. He either goes for a run or goes to work, leaving me and Sophie to enjoy the early morning quietude on our own.

"You're an early riser. You get that from me," he informs me with pride. "Your young man is an early riser too. He's already gone for a morning run."

"How do you know?" I ask.

It's weird to be in your forties and have someone

112

refer to someone else your age as young, but age is relative, I guess.

"I ran into him when I walked to the store to get a paper." Mitchell holds up the newspaper as evidence and looks at me over his reading glasses. "He was heading to his apartment after his ten kilometre run. He said he'll come over after he has a shower."

Eric isn't staying overnight while my dad and Zoe are here. He's worried my dad will think it's inappropriate.

I open the sliding glass door, and Sophie launches herself into the backyard like a missile.

"You can read the news online, you know," I remind him in jest.

"It's not the same," he insists, turning the page and snapping the paper.

"You're right," I agree. "The newspaper is less up-to-date than the online sources."

"Are you sure you want to have this debate, Bean?" he teases, chuckling. "Because I'm more than happy to spend the entire day convincing you."

"I know better than to debate with you," I say, picking up Sophie's bowls so I can refresh her water and fix her breakfast. "How did you sleep?"

"Like this." He drops his head to his shoulder, closes his eyes, and snores.

I roll my eyes. "Hilarious. I'll assume that means you slept well."

He couldn't have slept worse than me. I tossed and turned all night, worrying about his alibi situation. I return Sophie's bowls to the floor and open the back door. She bolts past me and runs straight to her breakfast.

We're alone. Maybe I should ask my dad where he was when Claire died. Maybe if I prepare him before Eric gets here, my dad will warm up to the idea of being questioned and cooperate.

"Dad." I swallow. He bends the top half of the newspaper toward him and looks at me.

"Yes, Bean?"

Sophie barks. I flinch. The front door opens and closes.

"Why are you so jumpy this morning?" my dad asks. "That's the second time you've startled in ten minutes."

"Good morning." Eric smiles. He's carrying a takeout tray with four coffees from Latte Da. He pulls one of the to-go cups out of the tray. "For you," he says, handing me the cup and kissing my forehead.

"Thank you." I crack the lid and inhale the comforting aroma.

I take a moment to savour the first sip of maple pecan latte and let the caffeine touch my soul while the warmth flows down my throat and emanates through my body. In the background, Eric explains to my dad he isn't sure what he and Zoe drink, so he got them each a medium roast and a bunch of coffee condiments on the side.

After a few minutes of awkward-for-me small talk, I announce I need to take Sophie for a walk, and my dad offers to join me. I thank him but decline his offer. Eric offers to join me in his place, and we tell my dad we'll leave him in peace to read his paper.

Coffees in hand, we step outside, and for the first time today, I feel like I can breathe. I inhale deeply and try to focus on the warm sun on my face and the birds singing their morning songs.

"You OK?" Eric asks. "It's like you're on pins and needles."

"I'm nervous," I explain, "and I didn't get much sleep."

"Are you worried about how your dad will react when I tell him I need to question him?"

I shake my head. "About his whereabouts when Claire was murdered." I take a moment to gather my thoughts. "What if his alibi isn't verifiable? What if you can't eliminate him as a suspect?"

"Heavy shoulders, long arms," Eric coaches me as we stop to wait while Sophie sniffs a fire hydrant.

Heavy shoulders, long arms is a mantra I learned in a yoga class in my twenties. I still use it today to remind myself to breathe and to release the tension in my neck and shoulders.

"I couldn't sleep last night, either," Eric admits. "Questioning them is just a formality. I'm sure I'll be able to eliminate him." The tension in his jaw and eye muscles when he forces a smile betrays the confident tone of his voice. He's trying to ease my stress about this situation.

"Thank you." I take his hand. "You're the best cop I've ever met. If anyone can prove my dad is innocent, it's you." I stand on my tippy toes and kiss him. "I know you're in a horrible position. You have my full support."

"The best way to eliminate Mitchell Monroe as a suspect is to find Claire's killer." He smiles and hugs me. "So that's what I'll do."

Agreed. That's what I intend to do too.

To PROCRASTINATE the unpleasantness of telling my father he's a suspect as long as possible, we walk twice as long as normal. Sophie must wonder what is going on. Her walks are extra long and extra frequent this week. She's loving the extra attention.

I'm not in a rush. The store will be slow today because the book fair is in full swing. I texted Connie and Marla last night to arrange for them to open the store, and cover for me, in case I'm late today. They assume I want to spend time with Mitchell and Zoe, and I didn't correct them. It's kind of true.

"Ready?" Eric asks, before he opens the door to the house.

"Ready." I nod.

"You're back!" Zoe gives us each a hug. "We weren't

sure whether to wait, so we ate without you. Can I get either of you some toast and half a grapefruit?"

"I already ate," Eric assures her, "but thank you."

"I'm not hungry," I add, my stomach in knots. I take a deep breath and pull up my proverbial big-girl pants. "Dad, we need to talk to you."

"Sounds serious, Bean." He takes his usual seat in the overstuffed chair in the living room. He pats his knee, and Sophie joins him, snuggling on his lap.

"It is," I confirm, sitting on the sofa cushion closest to his chair. Eric sits next to me, and Zoe sits across from us on the loveseat. "Why did you get a hotel room on Thursday instead of driving straight to Harmony Lake?"

He looks back and forth between Eric and me. "For days I ruminated over a plot hole in my manuscript, and the solution came to me while I was driving. Just like it always does," Mitchell explains. "I needed to capture my thoughts before I lost them, so I pulled over." He shrugs.

"This is how your father works, Megan. It's part of his process," Zoe elaborates. "I was the one who suggested the hotel. I knew your father would spend hours working. By the time he finished, it would've been late, and neither of us likes to drive at night if we can avoid it."

"We went to the hotel and checked in," Mitchell adds, picking up where his wife leaves off. "The Wi-Fi was as stable as a two-legged stool, and the room was uninspiring. Zoe stayed at the hotel, and I went somewhere with better Wi-Fi and more ambience."

Eric reaches into his pocket and pulls out his small notebook and a pen. He flips to the next open page of the notebook and clicks the top of the pen, then writes. This incites my dad.

"Wait," my dad says with his index finger in the air. He looks at me. "Are you questioning me, Bean?" He looks at Eric. "Is this an interrogation, Chief Sloane?"

"I need to ask you a few questions, sir," Eric says.

With my father rendered momentarily speechless from shock, Eric explains he needs to ask my dad about his absence from the hotel. He tells them he can question them here, instead of the station, and offers to question them himself to ensure the utmost discretion and avoid the media finding out Mitchell Monroe is a person of interest.

"I want my lawyer," my dad proclaims.

Eric closes his notebook and clicks his pen closed. "Call them."

"He's at least a day away from here," my dad insists.

The doorbell rings. Sophie barks and jumps off my dad's lap. Zoe and I both startle. I excuse myself to answer the door.

"Hello, Mitchell," Adam says. "I understand you need a lawyer."

Is he psychic? How could he know my dad just demanded to talk to his lawyer?

"Who called you?" Mitchell demands, sounding just as dumbfounded as I am.

"I did," Zoe replies.

"Why?" My dad and I ask in stereo.

"How did you know Dad would need a lawyer?" I ask her.

"I didn't." Zoe shrugs. "I asked Adam for advice about the internet lies," she explains. She looks at my dad. "I saw some online comments and conjecture yesterday. I didn't tell you because I didn't want to upset you. I asked Adam what we can do to minimize the damage to your reputation. He offered to come by this morning and talk to me. I assumed you'd be writing, so I didn't bother to tell you he was coming over. But with the brouhaha this morning, I forgot he was coming." She raises her eyebrows and leans toward her husband. "Wasn't it nice of Adam to offer to help us, Mitchell?"

"Why do I sense something bigger is going on?" Adam asks, lowering himself onto the loveseat next to Zoe. He surveys our blank stares. "Care to fill me in, Meg?" he asks, glaring at me.

"Your replacement, here, thinks I killed Claire Rivera!" Mitchell blurts out before I can answer.

"Mitchell!"

"Dad!"

Zoe and I admonish him in unison for his rude comment.

I gasp and use my scowl to reprimand him further for referring to Eric as Adam's replacement.

I look at Adam. "Eric needs to ask Dad a few questions, but he wants to wait for his lawyer who is far, far away," I summarize curtly.

"I see," Adam nods and sits back. He laces his fingers together and rests his hands on his lap. "Mitchell, would you like me to represent you while Eric questions you?"

"No, thank you!" my dad snaps. "I have a lawyer. He's just not here." He huffs. "Yet," he adds.

"I'd like you to represent me while I'm questioned, Adam," Zoe interjects.

"Zoe!" Mitchell exclaims. He draws his brows so close together they almost touch.

"What, Mitchell?" Zoe asks in a calm voice. "I have no desire to draw out this fiasco any longer than necessary. If answering Eric's questions will help him find Claire's killer sooner rather than later, he has my full cooperation."

"Coffee, Adam?" I ask, standing up. Sensing an opportunity, Sophie jumps onto the sofa and takes my spot.

Adam nods, so I excuse myself to the kitchen to take my time making the slowest coffee ever and give Zoe, my dad, and Adam an opportunity to talk alone.

"Well, this couldn't have gone worse," Eric says, following me into the kitchen.

"I'm sorry about what my dad said," I say to Eric as

I pull the crock pot out from under the sink and hoist it onto the counter. "It was inexcusable. And not true."

"I know, babe. He was angry. People get defensive and offensive when they feel cornered by the police," Eric justifies.

"It doesn't matter," I respond. "Don't make excuses for him. What he said was unacceptable." I plug in the crock pot and turn it on, then I drop a pod in the coffeemaker and turn it on too.

I place a mug under the spout, then get the meatballs out of the freezer.

"What are you making?" Eric asks.

"Sweet and sour meatballs," I reply. "For the family dinner tonight. It's potluck."

"This might be the most awkward family dinner ever," he mutters.

I sweeten Adam's coffee with cream and sugar, then pour a jar of sweet and sour sauce over the meatballs, and close the lid on the crock pot.

"Good news," Adam announces as he enters the kitchen. "They both agree to answer questions. I'll represent them. They'd like Meg to be present." He smiles, accentuating the lines around his blue eyes, and scratches the back of his head, mussing his hair.

"Thank you, Adam," I say, handing him his coffee. "I'm sorry we dragged you into this."

He winks. "Life is more exciting than fiction when Mitchell comes to town." He sips his coffee and looks at Eric. "Dude, you will be so dead this time next year."

He puts down his coffee and rubs his hands together. "How do you think Mitchell will kill you?" He chuckles, then adds, "In the literary sense, I mean. In a book. He'll kill you in a book."

I wish Claire's murder was a plot in a Mitchell Monroe book. Unlike real life, his books always end with the good guy figuring out whodunit and the culprit suffering the consequences of their evil deeds.

CHAPTER 14

WE REGROUP in the living room, and Eric starts by asking Zoe what she did while my dad was out. She claims she stayed in the room and watched a movie. The movie rental should appear on their hotel bill, and her cardkey should verify that she didn't leave the room.

"Also, my cell phone was on the entire time, so you'll be able to trace its location, right?" she asks Eric.

That was easy. I doubt questioning my dad will be as straightforward.

"Where did you go when you left the hotel, Mr. Monroe?" Eric asks.

My dad looks at Adam. Adam nods, and my dad looks at Eric.

"Some coffee shop not too far from the hotel."

"What was it called?"

Mitchell shrugs. "I can't remember."

"Did you keep a receipt?"

"I paid cash."

This is going nowhere.

"Describe the coffee shop, Dad. What was the first thing you noticed when you walked in?" I ask.

"It was one of those trendy places," he recalls. "It smelled like gourmet coffee and all the customers were on their laptops, cell phones, tablets, or all three. Most of the drinks had pretentious, hard-to-pronounce names."

"What did you order?" I ask, opening the internet browser on my phone and searching for coffee shops within a two-hour radius.

"I had two London Fogs and two cranberry biscotti. They had two menus, one vegan and one regular. I ordered from the regular menu. The manager recognized me from my book jacket and gave me the second London Fog and biscotti on the house." He sounds pleased with the amount of detail he's able to recollect.

"Tell us about the manager," I encourage, adding *vegan menu options* to my online search criteria.

"I wouldn't have known he was the manager if he didn't tell me. He wore the same black apron as his employees, and everyone was the same age. You know the type, well educated, overqualified, and full of existential angst." He gestures vaguely. "Typical young people."

I add *black apron* to my search criteria. The list is

getting shorter. There are a surprising number of trendy coffee shops around.

"Did the manager have a nametag?" Eric asks.

"Yes!" Mitchell replies with enthusiasm and snaps his fingers. "And he introduced himself to me. We shook hands, and he asked if I would take a selfie with him." He bites his lip while he thinks. "What was the boy's name?" The boy is probably in his thirties.

"Did you take the selfie?" Eric asks.

"Yes," Mitchell replies. "I try to be approachable and friendly. It's important to me to accommodate my readers."

I close the internet browser on my phone and open a social media app. I type in #MitchellMonroe. Wow, my dad wasn't kidding. It looks like he takes a selfie with anyone who asks. There are pages of photos of him posing with random people. I filter the results by date and look at the most recent posts first.

"He had one of those man-buns that have become so popular." He holds his hand on top of his head to show us where the coffee shop manager's man-bun was. "And those earrings you can see through. You know where they train their earlobes to have holes in them?" Mitchell snaps his fingers again. "He had two last names. *Ooof!* What was his name? It's on the tip of my tongue."

"He had a hyphenated last name?" Zoe probes.

"No," Mitchell clarifies. "His first and last names were both common surnames."

"Does Smith Wilson sound familiar?" I ask, turning my phone toward my dad.

He raises his reading glasses to his face and looks at my phone. "That's him!" he shouts like he just won a game of bingo. "Well done, Bean!" We high five. "She gets her resourcefulness from me," he announces to no one in particular.

I tilt the phone screen so Eric can see it. "Smith Wilson is the manager at The Daily Grind." I flash a smug smile, pleased with my aptitude for online stalking.

I take a screenshot of Smith Wilson's post, just in case he deletes it or makes his account private or something.

"The Daily Grind! That was it!" Mitchell confirms. He looks at Zoe. "It's one of those hipster places with clusters of sitting areas. There are sofas, chairs, coffee tables. They look like leather, but they aren't leather. All the sitting areas have signs explaining the furniture is vegan leather. Vegan leather!" He huffs. "Vegan leather is an oxymoron. Just call it plastic, for goodness' sake...."

While my dad expounds the absurdity of referring to anything not sourced from an animal as leather, I clear away the takeout cups and Adam's mug. Eric follows me into the kitchen, typing on his cell phone.

"This should be easy to verify," he assures me. "If all goes well, I'll text you in a couple of hours to tell you we eliminated Mitchell Monroe as a suspect in Claire's death."

"Thank you," I say, hugging him.

"I have to get going." He kisses the top of my head. "I'll pick you up at closing time?"

"Perfect." I kiss him goodbye.

He says goodbye to my dad, Zoe, and Adam as I check the crock pot before I leave.

"Meg, I'm leaving," Adam says, looking at his watch as he enters the kitchen. "I'm on mayor duty today. I have to attend a luncheon at the town hall with the book club, have my photo taken with Jules Janssen at her book signing, then go to the library and read *If You Give a Mouse a Cookie* to The LitWits."

The LitWits is a reading group for local children at the Harmony Lake library.

"Busy day," I comment. "I hope you have time to come for dinner." Adam says he'll be here for dinner but won't have time to make anything for the potluck, so he'll bring wine. "The most important part of any meal," I quip. "I'll walk you to the door."

My dad and Zoe are already at the door.

"Thank you for your help, Adam." Zoe kisses Adam's cheek, then discreetly nudges my father's ribs.

"Thank you, Adam. We appreciate your time and expertise." My dad extends his hand.

"Don't thank me yet. You haven't seen my bill." Adam winks.

Zoe and I laugh, but Mitchell isn't amused.

"He's kidding, Dad," I assure him.

"Of course, he is," Mitchell chuckles. "I know that."

They shake hands, which is the closest thing to affection I've ever seen them share, then Adam and I exchange a double-cheek kiss, and he leaves.

I look at the time and realize it's almost lunchtime. Connie and Marla are working a half day today, and I have to relieve them. Zoe suggests we go together since she's going to Knitorious to meet Connie. They plan to wander around the book fair together, then go back to Connie's place and cook for the pot luck tonight.

Mitchell asks if Sophie can stay with him. He says she's the perfect writing companion, good company without being demanding or distracting.

"You should write her into one of your books," Zoe suggests. "What book wouldn't be improved by a loyal animal companion?"

"You're right," I agree.

APRIL: *Dina Langley has been here all morning.*

Me: At the bakery?

April: Yup. Working on her laptop. She really likes lemon meringue tarts.

Me: Who doesn't? T's lemon meringue tarts are the best! Has Dina said anything?

April: She says lots of things. She's chatty and outgoing. Nothing about Claire's murder, though.

The *Familia*-inspired needle-felt display was popular this morning. We sold at least half of the figures. I'm rearranging the leftover items so the display looks less sparse when my phone dings again.

April: Dina just left. She's meeting Brooks Wiley for lunch. Can you talk?

I scan the store, even though I know I'm the only person here.

Me: Yes! The store is empty.

Moments later, my phone rings. I put April on speaker while I dig out my AirPods from the bottom of my purse.

"Hello?"

"Hi, Megapop! Not that it's a surprise, but T and I are bringing dessert to the potluck tonight."

"I figured," I say, popping my AirPods into my ears. "What are you bringing?"

"Nanaimo bars and toffee pecan shortbread."

"Mmm…" Just hearing the words make my tummy rumble.

"Dina just left," April informs me. "She got here just after we opened. She said she gets lonely in her hotel room by herself, and Eric asked her not to leave town, so she's trying to make the best of it."

"You and I are the only people she knows in Harmony Lake," I remind April. "It must be hard for her being stuck in a strange town by herself."

"He's not local, but she also knows Brooks Wiley.

When she packed up to leave, she said she was meeting him for lunch."

"Interesting," I think out loud.

"What's interesting?"

"I got the sense they don't like each other."

"I guess things change when you're both stuck in the same small town," April suggests.

"You're right," I agree, wondering if Brooks and Dina could be closer than they let on. I've caught him sneaking around with Jules, maybe sneaky relationships are his thing.

"She typed frantically for twenty-five minutes, then rewarded herself with a lemon meringue tart," April reports. "Then she typed frantically for twenty-five minutes again, then ate another tart. All morning."

"My dad does that when he's writing," I respond. "He says it's part of his process."

"Eats a lot of lemon meringue tarts?"

"No, the frantic typing-thing," I clarify. "He writes uninterrupted for twenty minutes, then takes a five-minute break and does something he likes. He calls the frantic typing sessions, sprints."

"I guess non-writers do sprints too," April surmises.

"What was she doing?" I ask.

"She said she was replying to social media posts and condolence emails from fans who reached out about Claire's death," April mumbles with her mouth full.

"What are you eating?" I regret skipping breakfast.

"Chocolate croissant," she replies, swallowing. Then takes another bite. "Why? You want some?" she garbles.

"Yes. I'm starving. This morning was a fiasco, and I missed breakfast."

"I'll be there in two minutes. I want to know everything."

Before I can respond, April ends the call.

True to her word, two minutes later, the bell over the door jingles, and April swoops in carrying my favourite box: a white confectionery box with the Artsy Tartsy logo on the lid.

"Thank you," I say, taking the box from her. "You're saving me from an afternoon of hunger." I bite into a croissant and let my eyes roll back in my head. "I can't leave because I'm alone until closing time," I mumble with my mouth full of flaky pastry goodness.

"Business is dead," she informs me. "Everyone is at the book fair today. The only customers we've had want the bookish cookies and nothing else."

"It's the same here," I agree, using the half-eaten croissant in my hand to point to the needle-felt display. "The felted *Familia* figures are the only thing we've sold today." I shrug and take another bite of croissant.

"So…" April makes herself comfortable in the cozy sitting area. "Who do you think killed Claire Rivera? I know you've been sleuthing."

Swallowing a mouthful of croissant, I join her on the sofa. "I don't know," I admit. "A few people have motives. Eric is verifying alibis to determine who also had opportunity."

"Who do you think did it?" I ask.

"Dina Langley," April replies without hesitation.

"Why?" I ask.

"First, she was there when it happened. Second, she had access to Claire to give her whatever nut product was the murder weapon," April alleges.

"Makes sense," I agree, taking another croissant from the box and closing the lid. "But the employment contract Dina had with Claire stipulated that Dina's job as Claire's assistant ends the day they release the last *Familia* book. Why would she make herself unemployed sooner?"

"Hmm," April ponders, "that strengthens my case. Dina would be unemployed either way." She shrugs. "She had nothing to lose."

Ding!

A knot of panic swells in my belly when my phone dings. What if it's Eric telling me he couldn't verify my dad's alibi?

CHAPTER 15

"Please let it be good news," I wish out loud as I pick up my phone from the counter.

Eric: He's eliminated! Do you want to tell him or shall I?

I let out a long, audible sigh of relief.

Me: Good job, honey! I'll let you deliver the good news.

"Good news?" April asks. "You look like a two-tonne weight just lifted off your shoulders."

I smile and nod, then return to the sofa and tell her about Mitchell going AWOL from his hotel room on Thursday, ending up on Eric's suspect list. I try to convey how awkward it is to watch your boyfriend question your father about a murder while you and your ex-husband try to support both of them.

"That explains why you missed breakfast," April

sympathizes. "We all knew Mitchell didn't kill Claire," she reassures me. "Now everyone else knows too."

"I know," I agree, nodding. "But I want to eliminate any possibility of doubt. The only way to do that is to find the killer."

"Just be careful." April's tone is serious, and her smile is tight and forced. "I don't want to embrace my inner sleuth to solve your murder."

She puts her hand on top of mine. I smile.

"Getting back to your theory that Dina is the killer," I say, guiding us back to our original conversation. "If Dina is the murderer, why was she afraid to be at the cottage after Claire died?"

"She was probably scared of Piper," April reasons. "From what you told me about this Piper person, she's not a good example of mental stability. With Claire dead, Dina likely worried Piper might shift her crazed obsession from Claire to her."

"Dina was terrified of Piper at the cottage yesterday," I reminisce. "You can't fake that kind of fear. It was real. I felt it."

"You think Piper killed Claire, don't you?" she asks.

"I did," I admit. "But now I'm not sure."

"What changed your mind?"

"A few things," I reply. "Piper is a huge *Familia* fan. If she killed Claire, there could never be a *Familia* revival, prequel, sequel, crossover series, or anything. Also, with Claire dead, Piper could never change her mind about retiring the series. You can't convince a dead person," I assert. "And Eric said when he questioned Piper, he had a hard time convincing her Claire was dead. He said Piper insisted Claire's death was a media hoax, or a publicity stunt, or something. If she was there when Claire died, how could she delude herself about it?"

"Maybe Piper was pretending she didn't believe Claire was dead, so she could claim mental incompetence if they caught her," April theorizes. My best friend has a knack for coming up with conspiracy theories; it's kind of her super power.

The bell over the door jingles, bringing our conversation to a premature end.

At first, it's difficult to make out her face through the black veil, but when we make eye contact, I recognize her.

"Speak of the devil," I mutter under my breath.

As I motion to get up, April touches my knee, and I look at her.

"Is that Piper?" she mouths.

I nod and get up.

"Hi there," I say, mustering my most cheerful voice and smile.

"Hello, there! You must be Megan Martel. I'm Piper Peters." She extends her gloved hand and smiles.

The bubbly voice is a stark contrast to her traditional Victorian-era mourning dress. Yes, mourning dress. Piper is wearing a floor length, black dress with long sleeves and a full skirt. The bodice buttons up to just underneath her chin where it's fastened with a cameo brooch. A black veil is draped over her black bonnet–yes, bonnet–obscuring her face.

All she needs is a black parasol and a case of the vapours, and I'd swear she just time-travelled here from 1850 England.

"Hi, Piper." I shake her gloved hand. "It's nice to meet you." Her black gloves feel like cotton. "Have we met before?" I ask, narrowing my eyes and tilting my head to one side. "You look familiar."

I don't know if she remembers me from the cottage yesterday, but I want to give her the opportunity to mention it without confronting her. I get the feeling it's a bad idea to confront Piper or back her into a corner.

"Yes," Piper responds. "I believe you were at Claire Rivera's cottage yesterday. We weren't formally introduced, but I never forget a face." She giggles.

Neither do I. Especially when we make eye contact through the window of a police car.

"I'm April." April extends her hand, and Piper shakes it.

I'm distracted by Piper's presence and didn't know April was behind me. I don't blame her for coming over for a closer look. Piper's attire is a lot to take in for the observer. Heck, I'm tempted to take a picture.

She must've brought the outfit with her. I can't think of anywhere local that sells this style of clothing. Is it a costume for the book fair? Some book fair attendees are cosplaying today, so maybe Piper is one of them.

Cosplay is a word fans use to describe wearing costumes and accessories to represent a certain character. I learned it from Hannah.

"It's lovely to make your acquaintance, April. I'm Piper Peters."

"Your dress is beautiful. The attention to detail is incredible," April compliments. "Who are you supposed to be?"

"Excuse me?" Piper asks, tilting her veiled head to one side.

The sudden corrugation on her forehead and the hint of offense in her voice makes me think Piper isn't cosplaying; this is a legitimate mourning outfit.

I'm about to give April a discreet prod under the counter before she says anything else that Piper might find insulting, but I'm too slow. My finger pokes her hip just as she says, "You're dressed as a literary character, right?"

"I most certainly am not!" Piper barks. "I am in mourning!"

From the shocked expression on her face, I can tell April gets it now. "I'm sorry for your loss," April sputters. "Mourning attire isn't very common in Harmony Lake."

Or in the twenty-first century, but I digress.

"Mourning attire signals to the world that a woman has suffered a significant loss." Piper reaches under her veil and dabs her eyes with a handkerchief.

"Would you like to sit down?" I offer. Piper nods,

and I gesture toward the cozy sitting area. "Would you like some water?"

"No, thank you," Piper replies, tucking her handkerchief into the cuff of her sleeve. When she sits, the spread of her skirt takes up the entire loveseat. "I've learned the hard way that when one is in mourning, it's best to avoid drinking anything unless absolutely necessary." She sighs. "You wouldn't believe how difficult it is to pee whilst wearing this dress," she overshares. "Very few public washrooms nowadays are spacious enough to accommodate a bustle."

I can't help myself; I have to know. It's driving me crazy. "Did you buy your mourning dress somewhere local?"

"Heavens, no," Piper replies. "When travelling, I always pack mourning attire. Just like the royal family, one must prepare oneself for any contingency." She giggles.

I make a mental note to ask Eric if packing a nineteenth-century mourning outfit constitutes premeditation.

I want to ask her what other contingencies she's prepared for, but I stop myself.

"Are you a knitter, Piper?" April asks.

"No," Piper retorts, vexed. "Why would you ask me that?"

I guess she hasn't forgiven April for thinking her dress is a costume.

"This is a knitting store," I explain. "Most people come here for yarn and knitting supplies."

"Right," Piper says, looking around and taking in the store from behind her veil. "I didn't realize."

"What brings you here today?" I ask, smiling and being as non-threatening as possible.

"Well, I was wandering through the exhibits at the book fair, and I noticed several people with small, felted figurines from the *Familia* books. I stopped one person, and she graciously told me you were selling them here. She even gave me your name."

"Yes, we sell them here." I gesture to the display. "A local artisan handcrafted each character and location," I explain. "One hundred percent of the proceeds will benefit a non-profit organization that supports community-based literacy programs…"

"I'll take whatever you have left," she interrupts my sales spiel.

"Oh," I say, shocked. "Would you like a closer look? Or the price of each item before you decide?" I ask.

"No, thank you." Piper smiles. "I'll take them." She giggles. "Please pack them such that they will endure a cross-Atlantic voyage."

She makes it sound like she'll be sailing back to England on the Titanic.

"I'll help you wrap them up, Megnolia," April offers, already pulling out tissue paper from under the counter.

"Oh, is your full name Magnolia?" Piper asks. "Magnolia is a lovely name."

"No," I correct her. "My name is Megan. April just likes to change it up, sometimes." She looks disappointed my name isn't Magnolia. "Were you and Claire close?" I ask.

April shoots me a look that silently screams, *What are you doing? Don't poke the bear!* I remove a price tag from the bottom of a needle-felted church and hand the church to April for packaging.

"Yes," Piper replies. "Our connection was deep. So deep it transcended the necessity for written words and verbal communication."

I'd bet my yarn stash that the restraining order Claire had against her is the real reason they didn't share written words or verbal communication.

"It sounds like a very special relationship," I sympathize, handing April a felt Mama and sticking the price tag to the counter.

"Yes," Piper agrees, "our souls were old friends."

A lovely sentiment that sounds ominous when she says it.

She wanders toward the back of the store.

"Were you shocked when Claire announced she was retiring *Familia*?" I shout so Piper can hear me. She's hovering near the back room.

"I didn't kill her, you know," she snaps as if one of us accused her. "What's in here?" She gestures to the back room. "Are there more felt figurines in here?" Her voice is now sweet and calm.

"Just a kitchenette, a back door, and some stairs," I assure her.

"She scares me," April whispers.

I nod.

"Do you want this one too?" I ask, holding up a tiny figure she won't be able to see from the back of the store through her veil.

"I want all of them," Piper reiterates.

She's distracted from the back room; mission accomplished. She walks toward the front of the store, craning her neck to look at the figure.

"Well done," April commends me.

"Thank you," I whisper.

"I know everyone thinks I killed Claire, but I didn't," Piper says matter-of-factly.

"We don't think you killed Claire," I say, trying to comfort her, though this interaction has moved her way up on my suspect list. "You're one of Claire's biggest fans, why would you harm her?"

"I'm not one of her biggest fans," Piper corrects me. "I am Claire Rivera's biggest fan! Why would I kill her? It would eliminate any chance of reading a new *Familia* book ever again!"

Her voice hitches on the last few words, and she pulls her handkerchief from her sleeve and dabs her eyes.

April finishes packing the felted items, and I ring up

the sale. After Piper pays, I thank her for her business and put her receipt in the bag.

"May I ask you one more question?" I ask, handing her the bag across the counter.

"Of course," Piper replies.

"How did you know where Claire and Dina were staying? Their location wasn't public knowledge."

"A kind lady told me," Piper says. "I was in line at the library to get my free Between the Covers Book Fair swag bag, and she was behind me. She asked if I planned to attend Claire's book signing. I told her that of course I would. Claire's book signing is the reason I came to the book fair. Then she told me she knows where Claire is staying. She even gave me directions."

"Do you remember her name?"

"We didn't exchange names," Piper replies, her veil swaying when she shakes her head.

"What did she look like?" I ask.

"It's hard to tell from the way she dressed," Piper explains with a one-shoulder shrug. "Not very tall, about your height. Baseball cap. Black backpack. Ginger-ish hair, I think. It was under her cap, so I can't say for sure."

"Lots of teeth?" I ask.

"Yes, now that you mention it. And her teeth were very white and very straight."

While April tells her about the *Familia*-inspired bookish cookies at Artsy Tartsy, I rush around the counter and hold the door for Piper. She thanks us for

142

our time and help, and we wish her a good day. After her bustle has cleared the threshold, I close the door behind her.

"Lock it!" April hisses.

"I'm glad you were here," I lock the door and turn the sign to CLOSED for a few minutes so April and I can regroup. "I don't think I could do that scenario justice if I described it to you."

"I'm glad I was here too," April responds. "If she'd snapped, she could only kill one of us at a time. The other one could run for help."

"Why did you send her to the bakery?" I ask.

"T needs to share this experience with us. Otherwise, she'll think we made it up or accuse us of exaggerating."

"Fair point," I say.

"Can I change my answer?" April asks.

"Answer to what?"

"To who killed Claire Rivera," April clarifies. "I'd like to change my answer to Piper Peters."

I'm leaning toward that answer too.

CHAPTER 16

TIME PASSES SLOWLY WITHOUT CUSTOMERS. I'm out of things to do. I've dusted, swept, mopped, tidied, and packed the online orders to drop off at the post office. With three hours left until it's time to close the store, I sit down with my needle-felting project. I just need to finish Sophie's ears and face.

I'm about to open the camera roll on my phone and look at a photo of Sophie to make sure I get her markings correct, when the bell jingles. Next thing I know, the real Sophie is in front of me with her front paws on my lap.

"Hey, Soph! This is a pleasant surprise." I detach her leash, and she trots toward the back of the store, no doubt en route to her water dish in the kitchenette.

"Hello, Bean!"

"Hey, Dad! What are you doing here?"

"It was time for a break. I'm craving another coffee

from Latte Da, so Sophie and I discussed it, and we decided to walk into town."

"How's your book coming along?" I ask.

"Slower than I'd like," he admits. "The manuscript is due at the end of the month, and I'm making some major last-minute changes."

"What kinds of changes?" I ask.

"It's time for Rock Granite to retire," my dad replies, then sighs like he's relieved to say it out loud.

"You're ending the series?" I stop stabbing and put down my felting needle so I don't stab myself by accident from the shock. "You're writing the last *Shark Attack* book? Ever?"

"That was the plan," he replies. "But our road trips to Toronto to visit Hannah, then to Harmony Lake to visit you have inspired me to go in a different direction." He winks. "I think I can keep the series fresh and still let Rock Granite enjoy his retirement."

"Wanna tell me about it?" I ask, knowing he won't give me any spoilers.

"You can wait and read it after it's published," he teases.

"Did Eric call you?" I ask, wondering if my dad knows Eric eliminated him as a suspect.

"He did better than that," he responds. "He stopped by the house to give me the good news in person. To say I'm relieved is an understatement."

"Listen, Bean," he says, sitting next to me on the sofa. "I owe you an apology. I'm sorry I was uncooperative and maybe rude earlier when you and Eric tried to question me." He shrugs one shoulder. "This is the first time I've been part of a real murder investigation. I panicked and got defensive. I shouldn't have said Eric was Adam's replacement. It was wrong."

"Thank you, Dad." I accept his apology. "I wasn't the only person hurt by your comment…"

"Yes, I know," he interjects. "I apologized to Eric when he came to the house."

"And?" I urge.

"And what?" he says, looking confused.

"Your comment was hurtful to Adam too. Don't you think you owe him an apology?"

He sighs. "I suppose."

"Maybe you could be nicer to Adam," I suggest. "We've been in each other's lives for over twenty years. He's Hannah's dad, and he's not going anywhere. It would mean a lot to me, and to Hannah, if you show him a little respect."

"It's not that I don't like Adam," my dad confesses. "It's just that I think marrying him held you back. If you didn't marry young, have a baby, and move here, you could've done great things."

"I did great things!" I throw up my hands in frustration. "Hannah is the greatest thing I've ever done. I have great friends. I have a great business. And I live in a great community. I have a great life. Adam didn't force this life on me," I enlighten him. "I wanted to live in a small town. I wanted to stay home with my daughter when she was young. Adam went along with my vision for our life, not the other way around." He appears shocked by this revelation. "And while we're on the subject," I add, "please be nicer to Eric than you were to Adam."

"I am nice to Eric," my dad says in his own defence, pulling himself up to his full-seated height.

"I don't mean tolerant and cordial," I clarify. "I mean, you need to give him a chance. He's a good person. I love him, and he's not going anywhere either."

Adam and Eric have different approaches for dealing with my dad. Adam gave up trying to impress my dad years ago. He accepted Mitchell would never feel warm and fuzzy toward him. Eric isn't like that. He won't give up. He'll drive himself—and me—crazy trying to impress my dad and win his approval.

"I understand, Bean," my dad concedes. "I'll do my best."

"Thank you," I say.

My dad and I should have had this conversation years ago. I should have stood up for Adam when we were married instead of two years after we split up. I won't make the same mistake with Eric.

"Now," my dad says, standing up and rubbing his hands together. "Can I leave Sophie here while I go to Latte Da and get another caffeine fix?"

"Of course," I say, glancing at Sophie who is sound asleep on her bed.

"Can I get you anything?"

"I'd love a maple pecan latte," I tell him. "Let me give you my loyalty card. I think my next coffee is free."

I pull out my purse from under the counter and rummage through it, looking for my wallet. Because my purse is a black hole of lost and forgotten items, I empty it item by item onto the counter. Keys... lip balm... sunglasses... knitting... tissues... business card. I stop and look at the business card. It's the one Brooks Wiley gave me when he asked me to pass his card along to my dad.

"Here." I slide Brooks's card across the counter toward my dad. "It's from Claire's agent, Brooks Wiley. He asked me to give it to you in case you're in the market for a new literary agent."

"I've already got one," my dad says, patting his breast pocket. "You can keep it." He slides the card back toward me.

"Where did you get Brooks Wiley's business card?" I ask.

"He gave it to me," my dad explains. "A few minutes before we got here. Sophie and I were walking through the park across the street, and Brooks walked up to us and introduced himself. I'm happy with my agent, but I took the card to be polite."

"Was Brooks alone?" I ask, wondering if he and Jules Janssen were having a secret rendezvous in the park.

"He was with a woman," my dad replies,

confirming my suspicion. "You should have seen her, Bean. She was wearing authentic 1800s mourning attire and eating one of the bookish cookies Tamara made." He shakes his head and gestures to his chest. "There were cookie crumbs all over her bodice."

Brooks Wiley hanging out with Piper Peters? If it weren't for my dad's accurate description of Piper's attire, I wouldn't believe it. There can't be two British women walking around Harmony Lake in mourning attire, can there? Yesterday, I watched Brooks run away from Piper and hide behind a police officer at the rental cottage. Why would he hang out with her in the park?

"Are you sure?" I ask, dumbfounded.

"About which part?" he asks back. "I'm certain about her outfit. I did a double take. It's not everyday you see a British woman in full period attire, Bean."

"How do you know she's British?" I ask.

"They were talking and laughing as Sophie and I walked past them," he explains. "Her accent was clear as a bell."

If they were laughing, it doesn't sound like Piper ambushed Brooks or was harassing him.

"Dad, did Brooks seem scared to you?"

"Scared?" he asks, astonished. "Scared of what? Of me?"

"No," I clarify. "Did he seem nervous about the woman he was with?"

"Not at all," my dad replies. "Like I said, they were laughing and smiling." He shrugs one shoulder. "They seemed to have a pleasant conversation. When I walked by, he excused himself from her and told her he'd be right back."

"Did you hear what they were talking about?"

He shakes his head. "No, but I wasn't eavesdropping, Bean. From what I hear about your sleuthing hobby, eavesdropping is more your thing than mine," he teases.

This is so strange, it's hard to believe. Maybe it wasn't Brooks?

"What did Brooks look like?" I ask, starting to sound like I'm interrogating my father.

"Handsome," he responds. "Expensive Italian suit, clean-shaven head... he has a unique accent. At first, I thought he was British, too, like his friend, but he has a distinct, Caribbean inflection."

Sounds like Brooks to a tee.

He kisses Jules Janssen in secret, has lunch with Dina even though he insinuates he doesn't like her, and now he's going for a walk in the park with Piper Peters, a woman he claimed to be frightened of yesterday. I need to talk to Brooks.

AFTER A LOVELY POTLUCK DINNER, everyone leaves with full bellies and containers of leftovers.

Adam was the last to leave and, to my and Zoe's

surprise, Mitchell offers to walk him to his car. Under the guise of finishing an already complete crossword puzzle, Zoe makes herself comfortable in the living room chair with the best view of the driveway. I think she's just as curious as me about Mitchell walking Adam to his car.

"Have you seen my laptop cord?" Eric asks. I shake my head and sink into the family room sofa. "I could've sworn it was here," he mumbles, checking all the outlets, in case the cord is plugged into one of them. "Maybe I left it at the office."

"You can use my laptop," I offer.

"Thanks, but I can't access work stuff on your laptop," he replies, sitting next to me. "I'll use my phone until I get to the office tomorrow." He unlocks his phone and opens his email. "The forensics team didn't find any traces of nuts on the items we confiscated from the cottage. How did the peanut oil get onto Claire's fingertips?" He blows out an exasperated breath.

"Maybe the killer took the murder weapon with them," I propose.

"That's what I assume," he responds. "I wish I had an inkling of what it might be. We've checked the woods around the cottage for clues, but we've found nothing. I was hoping the killer tossed the murder weapon into the trees when they left."

"I guess the killer didn't leave behind anything obvious like a hair or some fingerprints?"

"The forensics people only found two sets of finger-prints," he says. "Claire's and Dina's."

"Does that mean the killer wore gloves?" I ask.

Eric shrugs. "Either they wore gloves, or they didn't touch anything," he speculates.

He's looking at crime scene photos on his phone, and I'm looking at them, too, over his shoulder.

"How did the killer leave if the door was locked from the inside, and Claire had the only key?" I ask.

"The landlord says there's another key," Eric discloses. "It's missing. We contacted the people who rented the cottage before Claire and Dina, in case they accidentally took the second key with them when they left. They say they don't have it." He looks at me. "I think the killer took the key with them when they left, probably because it had their fingerprints on it."

"I assumed they left through the window," I say. "It's a large window, and it's on the main floor." I point to the photo on his phone. "The drapes are billowing in this photo. The window was open when you found Claire's body," I deduce.

"That's the other theory," Eric admits. "The window makes sense because the killer could avoid walking through the cottage, and Dina wouldn't see them because the window in the den faces the opposite direction from the dock where she was sitting. Or the killer waited inside the den until Dina came back to the cottage, then snuck out the window. This way they wouldn't risk bumping into her outside."

The thought of being that close to a murder-in-progress makes me shudder.

"I guess it's a good thing the second key was missing. If Dina found the spare key, she would've found Claire, and she would see that image in her mind's eye forever." Sadly, I speak from experience; finding a dead friend is something you can never unsee.

"Dina didn't look for the spare key," Eric explains. "She didn't know about the spare key. She said there was only one key when they arrived at the cottage over a week ago."

Did the killer plan Claire's murder far enough in advance to sneak into the cottage and steal the spare key before Claire and Dina even arrived?

"Why did Claire lock the door?" I wonder aloud. "Dina was the only other person there, and she was sitting by the dock. Claire didn't have to lock the door to be alone."

"Dina says Claire always locks herself away to work." He shrugs. "Apparently it's part of her creative process."

I guess it's not weirder than driving without a cell phone being part of my dad's creative process. But part of me wonders if Claire locking herself in the office is less related to her creative process and more related to Brooks's claim that Claire and Dina were having a loud argument that day.

"Did you ask the landlord about the spare key?" I ask.

Eric nods. "He says he was unaware the key was missing until I told him. But he also said he doesn't check for both keys when he inspects the cottage between renters. We asked the cleaner when she last saw the key, and she has no recollection." He lets out a frustrated sigh. "For all we know, that second key has been missing for months."

"Or the killer has it," I remind him.

"The other weird thing is we found more of Dina's fingerprints in the den than Claire's." He looks at me. "Does that seem odd to you? Dina said Claire used the den as her office, and she said Claire likes to work alone, in silence. Wouldn't you expect to find more of Claire's fingerprints than Dina's?"

I shrug, and I'm about to tell him I don't know when Zoe appears in the doorway.

"That doesn't sound odd to me," Zoe chimes in. "If the police investigated Mitchell's home office, I'm sure they'd find more of my fingerprints than his."

"Why?" Eric asks.

"Because even though I don't spend as much time in Mitchell's office as he does, when I'm in there I touch more stuff," she explains. "Mitchell sits at his desk and types. He touches a few things on and around his desk, but I'm the one who tidies up after him, restocks his supplies, and organizes the things he moved around."

I guess that makes sense. I wonder if the police investigated Knitorious, if they'd find just as many of Connie and Marla's fingerprints as mine?

CHAPTER 17

Sᴜɴᴅᴀʏ, April 18th

"Good morning, Bean!" my dad says without looking up from his laptop.

"Good morning, Dad. Do you always start work this early?" The sun just rose, and it looks like he's been hard at work for a while.

"Only when I'm up against a deadline," he replies with a chuckle. "I was just taking a break and reading some of Claire's online obituaries."

"Yes, there are some lovely articles about her life and career," I observe. "I read a few yesterday." I open the back door and let Sophie out, then freshen her water and fix her breakfast.

"Until today, I'd never read articles about her or interviews she gave," my dad explains. "It's strange... she said she always wanted to be an author. She said writing was her dream from the time she was a child."

"Why is that strange?" I ask.

"Because it's the complete opposite to what she told me when I hired her as my assistant," he replies. "The Claire Rivera I knew had no interest in writing. She wasn't even a keen reader. As I recall, she preferred gossip magazines and tabloid newspapers to books. She didn't study writing, she studied graphic design in college."

"Why would she lie to you?" I wonder out loud. "Maybe she thought you wouldn't hire an aspiring author?" I suggest.

He shakes his head. "Poppycock. I've mentored plenty of young authors," my dad insists. "I don't think Claire lied to me, I think she lied in all these interviews." He gestures to his laptop.

"Why?" I ask.

He shrugs. "Maybe her publisher's PR people thought it was a good idea," he offers.

"She also talked a lot about her needle-felting hobby in those interviews," I comment. "She said needle felting was such an important part of her life that she included it in her book series as the main character's hobby. Did you know Claire was a needle felter?"

My dad shakes his head and closes his laptop. "I never saw her do it, and she never mentioned it to me," he says, opening the back door so Sophie can come inside.

It's possible Claire discovered her love of needle felting after she quit as my dad's assistant.

"Dad, why are you certain Claire took your idea and turned it into the Familia series?"

"It's a bit of a coincidence that when Claire worked for me, I was in the planning stages of a books series about an organized crime family headed up by a matriarch who knits, then less than a year after she quit, she released the first *Familia* book," he alleges.

"Do you think she copied your computer files?" I ask. "Or did you talk to her about your idea?"

My dad shakes his head. "I never give my assistants access to my computer or my files," he insists. "And the only person I bounce ideas off is Zoe. I think Claire pieced it together by going through my notebooks and the notes I collect."

"Ah," I respond with a nod.

My dad likes to capture ideas as soon as they come into his head. He keeps notebooks around his house, in his car, and even in his pocket for this purpose. In the event he has an idea when there isn't a notebook within arm's reach, he'll jot it down on whatever is handy. A napkin, the back of an envelope, a sticky note. When I was ten years old, he stopped the car and jotted down a note on a ten-dollar bill.

"I'm convinced Claire lied to me, Bean." His face is clouded with sadness. "She must've planned to use me all along. It makes little sense, but that's the only explanation."

"Claire came to see me the day before she died," I

tell him. "She asked me to set up a meeting with you and her. She wanted to bury the hatchet."

We sit in silence while Mitchell takes a moment to contemplate what I said.

"I'm sad Claire died without resolving the issues between us, but I'm not sure I would have agreed to meet her, Bean," he admits.

There are too many inconsistencies between Claire Rivera, who worked as my father's author assistant, and Claire Rivera, the best-selling author. I can't help but think that hidden somewhere in all the inconsistencies is the reason someone wanted Claire dead.

"You got a waffle maker?" I ask, more excited than the sight of a countertop appliance should warrant. "I love waffles!" I approach the waffle maker on Adam's sleek and modern kitchen counter and open the lid.

"I know," he says. "You're the perfect guinea pig for me to try it out."

Every Sunday, Adam and I have brunch with our daughter, Hannah. Adam and I meet in person, and Hannah joins us by video chat. We alternate between his place and mine, but Adam always cooks. Since we split, Adam has become a culinary hobbyist, and I'm more than happy to let him cook brunch every week. Especially since I did all the cooking during our twenty-year marriage.

While Adam makes waffle batter, I cut up strawberries and prepare other waffle toppings.

"Thank you again for helping my dad and Zoe yesterday," I say, putting the strawberry pieces in a bowl. "I know Mitchell didn't seem appreciative, but he was."

"He thanked me last night," Adam says.

"When he walked you to your car after dinner?" I ask.

Adam nods. "Yup. He thanked me for helping him and Zoe yesterday, and he apologized for not liking me."

"That's how he said it?" I ask, shocked. "He said, I'm sorry for not liking you?"

"No, Meg. He was more sincere than that."

"Wow." I can't believe my dad apologized to Adam.

"He hugged me too."

"He hugged you?" I wipe my hands and sit down.

Adam nods. "I don't know what you said to him, Meg, but it worked. He's trying to make amends for over two decades of resentment and contempt."

"What makes you think I had anything to do with it?"

"Either you said something to Mitchell, or he's in the early stages of dementia," Adam replies.

"I asked him to be nice to you. I reminded him you're Hannah's dad," I confess. "And I might have cleared up a few misconceptions he had about our relationship." I open the fridge and find the whipped cream, then I look at Adam. "I regret not standing up for you sooner. I should've set Mitchell straight years ago, and I'm sorry I didn't."

"I don't think he would have been ready to hear it years ago," Adam says. "Mitchell needed someone to blame when you didn't choose the life he wanted for you, and I was the most logical choice."

"I get that now," I acknowledge, "and I cleared up his misconceptions."

"I bet he'll still kill me in his next book," Adam teases with a chuckle.

"Speaking of books," I say, changing the subject. "How was your photo op at Jules Janssen's book signing yesterday? I saw a photo of you and her on The Front Page. Are you starstruck?"

"I'm not starstruck, Meg," he replies, rolling his eyes at the suggestion that he could be awestruck by a gorgeous, charismatic, A-list celebrity. "Our meet and greet was short and sweet." We carry the waffles and toppings to the table. "She seemed friendly, but her handlers whisked her off as soon as the photographer got the shot. She mentioned she thinks Harmony Lake is a beautiful town, and she thinks it would be an ideal location for part of the *Familia* movie."

"I don't think there will be a *Familia* movie," I comment, picking up Adam's iPad and FaceTiming our daughter.

"That's what I said!" Adam agrees. "But Jules said she's optimistic. She said she just eliminated a major obstacle. She said she believes she's close to acquiring the movie rights."

Is it me, or does Jules' claim about eliminating a major obstacle sound like a confession?

While we eat waffles and drink fresh-squeezed orange juice, Adam and I have an enjoyable virtual visit with Hannah. She'll be home for the summer in less than two weeks. It's incredible how much I still miss her. I assumed I'd get used to her living away from home, since this is the end of her second year of university, but it's still hard to be so far away from her.

"I have to get to the store for Mitchell's book signing," I say after I help Adam clean the kitchen. "Thanks for breakfast."

"I'll see you there," he says. "I'm having my photo taken with him for The Front Page."

"I'll save you a copy of his latest *Shark Attack* book," I tease.

We exchange a cheek kiss, and I leave.

MITCHELL'S APPEARANCE is in thirty minutes, but there's already a line outside Knitorious when I arrive.

Knitorious is closed on Sundays and Mondays, but we're open today to host my dad's reading and book signing. He requested his appearance be at the store instead of the book fair venues.

"You're here early," I say when I walk through the

backdoor to find Mitchell, Zoe, and Connie sitting at the harvest table at the back of the store, drinking coffee and eating coffee cake.

Sophie rushes over to greet me, and I bend down to rub her.

"Your neighbour dropped off this beautiful arrangement," Zoe says.

"They're gorgeous." I inhale deeply to take in as much of the floral scent as possible.

"It's your April bouquet," Connie explains. "Phillip thought it would brighten up the store for the book signing."

Early in our relationship, Eric and I went to a fundraiser with a silent auction. One prize was a year of monthly floral arrangements courtesy of Wilde Flowers, the florist shop next door to Knitorious. Eric had the winning bid and every month for a year, I received a beautiful floral arrangement. When my year of floral arrangements expired, Eric renewed it as an anniversary gift, so now I'm enjoying another year of floral arrangements.

When it's time to start, there are more people in line than will fit in the store.

"Hi, Megan!"

"Hi, Lucas," I greet the rookie cop who's leaning against the wall on the sidewalk just outside the door. "What are you doing here?"

"Crowd control," he replies. "Chief Sloane sent me."

I'm not sure how to manage a crowd this size. We've never had so many people in Knitorious at once.

"I'm glad you're here." The relief is clear in my voice.

"Leave it to me," Lucas assures me. "This is nothing compared to the crowd yesterday at Jules Janssen's book signing. This is manageable."

Reassured by the young officer's confidence, I turn the sign from CLOSED to OPEN and step aside.

The store is full, and Lucas leans against the door, keeping it open, so the people who can't fit inside can hear as Mitchell reads an excerpt from his book, from the comfort of one of the overstuffed chairs in the cozy seating area.

After the reading, my dad moves to the harvest table. Lucas organizes everyone in an orderly line extending from the harvest table, out to the sidewalk, and down Water Street.

After Mitchell signs a book, I direct the person toward the back door and hand them off to Connie. She wishes them a good day and sends them on their way. Zoe is busy selling books and taking photos for people who want a picture with my dad.

We take a quick break when Adam, in his role as Mayor Martel, and the photographer from The Front Page show up. While Adam and my dad pose for a couple of photos, I see Brooks Wiley next in line to meet my dad and get his book signed.

"Hi, Brooks," I say.

"Nice to see you again, Megan." Brooks nods and smiles. "I'm here to meet Mitchell Monroe and ask him to sign my book." He holds up a copy of the latest *Shark Attack* book.

"I hear you met him yesterday in the park," I say.

"In passing," Brooks acknowledges with a grin. "I gave him my card."

"Did you have a pleasant walk through the park with Piper Peters?" I ask.

Guiding me by the arm, Brooks leads me away from the people waiting in line. Lucas asks me if everything is OK, and I assure him it is.

"It wasn't how it looked," Brooks hisses when we're in front of the display window.

"It looked like you were laughing and having fun with someone you insisted was scary and dangerous the day before."

"I was humouring her," he explains. "She's... fragile."

"Fragile?" I ask, confused. "Like a flower?" Fragile isn't the first word I'd use to describe Piper Peters.

"Fragile like a bomb," Brooks clarifies. "I was being careful. I didn't want to set her off."

It's a fair observation. I sensed Piper had a short fuse when she was at Knitorious yesterday with April and me.

"What did you and Piper talk about?" I ask, knowing it's none of my business and expecting Brooks to tell me so.

"We didn't." He shrugs one shoulder. "She'd just approached me when your dad walked past us. I used him as an excuse to get away from her."

"I thought maybe you and Piper were having a secret rendezvous in the park," I tease.

"Why would you think that?" he asks, chuckling.

"You meet Jules in secret." I quirk an eyebrow. "Maybe secret meetings are your thing."

"Who?" he asks, trying to convince me he doesn't know what I'm talking about.

"Jules Janssen," I specify.

"I know who she is. I don't know her personally," Brooks lies.

"It looked pretty personal when you were kissing her and groping her butt in the alley beside my store." I escalate my voice toward the end of my sentence.

"Shhh," he says, his brows furrowed together. "Keep your voice down, woman!" he hisses. "Fine, Jules and I are friends."

I stifle a giggle and raise my eyebrows.

"Good friends. We're quite close."

"Did Claire know about your close relationship with Jules?" I ask.

"She did not," Brooks confirms. "My personal relationships were none of Claire's business."

"Even when your personal relationship is with someone who's trying to buy the film rights to her books?"

"I don't like what you're insinuating," Brooks chal-

165

lenges. "I always worked in Claire's best interest. Selling the film rights to *Familia* was in her best interest."

Claire believed otherwise. But I don't argue with him.

Zoe comes over and tells Brooks it's his turn to meet Mitchell.

"I don't want to lose my place in line," he says, looking at me. "Excuse me, Megan."

After he gets his book signed and takes a selfie with my dad, I escort Brooks to the back door. I'm about to hand him off to Connie when he tilts his phone toward me.

"Look at this," he says. "These are some emails and letters Piper sent to Claire," he explains. "I want you to see how disturbed she is, so you'll know I'm telling the truth when I say I wouldn't meet her alone in a park."

I scroll through the emails on his phone. I can't spend much time looking at each one, but Brooks is right, they are disturbing. It seems Piper believed that her and Claire's lives were intertwined and that Claire used her books to share secret messages with Piper. Piper also thinks things Claire said in interviews, and even certain outfits or colours Claire wore, were secret messages to Piper. It's creepy, and it's enough to convince me to avoid being alone with Piper.

CHAPTER 18

TODAY, I'm thankful I sell yarn and not books; boxes of the former are much lighter than boxes of the latter. I'm lugging the last box of *Shark Attack* books from the storage room into the store when Dina flags me down from her place in line.

"Hi, Dina," I say, wiping box-dirt from my hands onto my jeans. "How are you?"

"I'm OK," she replies, hugging me. "Excited to meet Mitchell Monroe. He's one of my mentors! I wrote a paper on his creative process when I got my Master of Fine arts." She spins around and shows me the black backpack she's carrying. "I brought my *Shark Attack* books." She smiles. "I understand if he doesn't have enough time to sign all of them."

"That looks heavy." If every book in the series is in there, it weighs about twenty pounds. "Would you like me to put it by the table for you?"

Dina dismisses my offer with a wave of her hand. "It's fine. I'm a bookworm, I'm used to toting books everywhere." We laugh.

"If you were here earlier, you would've run into Brooks," I tell her.

"I've seen enough of Brooks this weekend," she says, shaking her head. "I don't need to see any more of him."

"Yes, I hear you had lunch together yesterday," I say.

"Yeah," she nods. "We went to the local pub. It was nice. They have excellent food. The Irish nachos are the bomb!"

"They are," I agree, suddenly craving a platter of Irish nachos. "Can I ask you something, Dina?" She nods, so I proceed. "I get the feeling you don't like Brooks. Why did you have lunch with him?"

"He said he needed to talk to me about Claire. He said it was important," she replies, not denying my allegation that she doesn't like him.

"Oh?" I urge.

Dina looks at the line of people behind her, then uses her chin to gesture to a quiet corner of the store. "If we step over there to talk, will I lose my place in line?"

I shake my head. "I'll make sure you don't."

Dina follows me toward the cozy sitting area.

"He wanted me to approach Claire's family and convince them to sell the *Familia* film rights to him and Jules Janssen," she whispers near my ear.

"Brooks wanted you to do that?" I clarify.

Her eyes are wide, and she gives me a deep nod. "He doesn't know Claire's family, but I do. They like me and I like them. He thought my relationship with them would give me an advantage."

"Did you agree to do it?" I ask.

"No! Of course not!" Dina sounds almost insulted. "I wouldn't take advantage of them in their time of grief. Even if they weren't grieving, I wouldn't do it. Claire was clear. She did not want *Familia* made into a movie or TV series."

"Good for you for doing what you felt was right," I commend her.

"He said they're going to approach Claire's family with or without me. If I helped them, they would've cut me in, but I don't care. I don't need the money bad enough to go against Claire's wishes or take advantage of her family's grief."

"They, who?" I ask. She looks at me confused. "You said they're going to approach Claire's family with or without you. Who are they?"

"Brooks and Jules," she replies. "They're partners."

Before I can ask her anything else, Zoe summons Dina to meet Mitchell and get her books signed.

While Mitchell and Dina talk, my back is to them as I empty the last box of books.

"Don't stab yourself," my dad teases with a jovial tone in his voice. "I guess that's one way to keep pick-pockets out of your stuff." He and Dina laugh.

I turn around to see what they're laughing about, but come face-to-face with a fan looking for Mitchell Monroe's previous books to purchase. By the time I refer him to Zoe, Dina and Mitchell finish their meet-and-greet, and I'm ushering Dina toward the back door.

"It was nice seeing you, Dina," I say as I gesture toward the back door. "Oops! You have a little something." I point to her shoulder. "May I?"

She nods, and I pick a piece of lime-green fibre fuzz from her shoulder. "A bit of fibre attached itself to you. It must be your magnetic personality," I tease, holding up the offending fluff.

Dina shrugs. "Well, I am in a yarn store." She giggles and waves goodbye on her way out.

Soon after Dina leaves, we run out of *Shark Attack* books. The empty boxes are strewn about the back room and kitchenette area because I've just been haphazardly tossing the boxes in there as I empty them. There hasn't been a spare second to tidy up.

Zoe announces to the fans waiting in line that we are out of books. A chorus of disappointed groans follows her announcement. She assures everyone that if they already have a book, they're welcome to wait and Mitchell will gladly sign it. The line reduces by half after the mass exodus of hopeful book buyers.

Only a few people remain when Piper Peters joins the end of the line. She's still grieving, as evidenced by the mourning attire she's wearing again today. I must be growing accustomed to her outfit, because I find it less shocking. Judging by the astonished expression on her face, this is Zoe's first time encountering Piper.

"Good afternoon, Piper," I greet her with a smile.

"Megan! How lovely to see you again." She extends her gloved hand toward me with her wrist limp and her fingertips facing the floor.

Unsure what to do with her extended, flaccid hand, I attempt a handshake and end up tugging her fingers.

"We're out of books, I'm afraid," I say, hoping this information will render her visit fruitless, and she'll leave.

"No worries," she assures me. "I brought my own." Her other hand produces a *Shark Attack* book from the multitude of folds in her full skirt.

"Awesome," I say as Zoe uses hand motions to beckon Piper to the harvest table.

I accompany Piper and stand nearby, keeping a close watch on their interaction, looking for signs that Piper's unhealthy obsession with Claire might transfer to my father.

Mitchell signs her book, poses for a selfie with Piper, and shakes her droopy, gloved hand. Zoe summons the next person in line while I usher Piper to the back room.

"Thank you for coming, Piper," I say when we reach Connie at the back door.

"It was a pleasure," Piper responds while Connie takes in her elaborate outfit. "Oooh, it's lovely back here," Piper comments, looking around the unremarkable, utilitarian back room. "What's in here?" She jiggles the handle of the storage room door.

"Yarn," I reply, guiding her gently by the arm toward Connie. "I had to remove most of the yarn from the store to make room for the books."

"Right. Of course," she responds. "Well, hello, there." Piper extends her limp hand toward Connie. "It's lovely to make your acquaintance. I'm Piper Peters." She grins beneath her veil.

Connie introduces herself, then shakes Piper's wilted hand, and uses it to lead her through the back door. "Have a wonderful day, Piper. Thank you for coming." Connie closes and locks the back door behind her.

Back in the store, my father is walking around, stretching his legs, and shaking out his right hand, which is probably cramping after signing several hundred books this afternoon.

I'm itching to lock the door, but one person is loitering near the front of the store, leafing through a knitting magazine.

I turn the sign from OPEN to CLOSED and thank Lucas for helping with crowd management.

"No problem, Megan," the rookie officer responds. "Enjoy the rest of your afternoon," he says before leaving.

From a distance, I watch the lone patron thumb through the latest issue of Vogue Knitting magazine and stare at the back of their head, using my non-exis-tent powers of telepathy to will them to leave.

"Gross habit," my dad whispers in my ear.

I look at him, baffled. "What's a gross habit?" I whisper.

"Licking your fingers before turning the page," he specifies, glaring at the finger-licker. "And it's unaccept-able when it's a magazine you don't own."

I nod. "It's a gross habit," I agree.

"Claire used to do that," he whispers, watching the finger-licker. "She couldn't turn a page without licking her thumb and forefinger first. I would look away when she did it because it grossed me out." He gestures vaguely in the general direction of nostalgia. "I remember warning her she'd catch a cold or worse, either from licking her dirty fingers, or from picking up whatever germs are lurking on the corners of the pages. But she never listened."

"You're right," I say, struck with an epiphany. "A person could catch a cold or flu because of that habit."

I bet they could pick up other things too. I think I just found the murder weapon that killed Claire, or at least narrowed down the options.

At last, the lone remaining customer closes Vogue Knitting, and as they motion to pick up another maga-zine, Zoe opens the front door, distracting them with the jingle of the bell, and wishes them a good day. Taking the polite hint, the customer leaves.

"WHERE IS EVERYONE?" Eric asks, looking deflated.

"Who?" I ask.

"Your dad, Zoe, all the people who want to get their books signed?" He crouches down and greets Sophie, who's wagging her entire back end because she's so happy to see him.

"Gone," I update him. "We ran out of books, so the signing ended early."

"I came to help, but I guess I'm too late. I thought we could take your dad and Zoe out for dinner." He looks around, surveying the empty boxes laying haphazardly around the back room.

When Eric kisses me hello, I sense his tension. His facial muscles are taut, and his body is more rigid than usual when he hugs me.

"Dad and Zoe are having dinner with Connie and Archie," I explain. "Then they're going to Connie and Archie's place to play euchre. If I'd known you were coming…"

"It's not your fault." He lets out an exasperated sigh. "I messed up this visit. I wanted to get to know your dad and Zoe. I booked the weekend off work to help with the book fair. Then this murder happened, and instead of making a good impression with your family, I'm interrogating your father, chasing witnesses all over town, and trying to get straight answers about anything."

"Honey, it's fine," I assure him. "You made a great impression. Everyone understands. A murder investigation takes priority over a book fair."

"I can't keep these witnesses in town forever, babe. I need to solve this case before they scatter and go back to where they came from." He watches me toss another flattened box onto the pile. "Let me help you put the store back together," he offers, picking up a box. "It's the least I can do, and it might be the only thing I accomplish today."

I take the box from him and toss it aside. "Maybe I can improve your day," I tease.

"I'm listening," he says.

The tone of his voice is serious, but the glint in his eye when he cocks his eyebrow and smirks tells me we have different ideas about how to improve his day. Focus, Megan!

"What would you say if I told you I have a theory about how Claire ingested the peanut oil?"

"I'd apologize in advance for hugging you so hard you might break in half," he jokes. "Wait. Are you serious?" he asks, straightening his spine. "You figured out how Claire was poisoned?"

"I think so," I reply. "Maybe," I add to manage his expectations in case I'm wrong. "When Claire was here, she was flipping through a pattern book..."

I continue, telling him about Claire's habit of licking her thumb and finger with each page turn, and how my dad mentioned it was a habit she had back when she was his assistant. I tell him Mitchell's theory that such a habit is an effective way to catch a cold.

"If you can pick up a cold, you can pick up other things too. Like peanut oil," Eric surmises, coming to the same conclusion I did.

"Exactly," I concur.

"Babe, that's brilliant!" He wasn't kidding about hugging me tight. He lets go when I gasp for air. "But we checked every book in the den for traces of nut products."

"My dad says Claire preferred magazines to books," I tell him.

Eric unlocks his phone, and his thumbs move across the keyboard so fast they're practically a blur. "I'll send a team to confiscate every book, magazine, and piece of paper in the cottage, not just the den. We'll check all of them for traces of peanut oil."

It's ironic that a book, something Claire claimed to love and is her legacy, might be the instrument of her demise.

While he types and sends instructions to his team, I attach Sophie's leash and put on my jacket.

"I'm going to walk Sophie." I kiss him goodbye.

"Wait, I'll come with you." He finishes typing, sends a message, and shoves his phone in his pocket. "Let's order dinner, and we can walk Sophie together before it gets here," he suggests.

"Aren't you going back to work?" I ask.

"We haven't seen each other all day," he reminds

me. "What do you feel like for dinner?" he asks, holding the door for Sophie and me.

"I've been craving Irish nachos since Dina mentioned them earlier," I confess, stepping into the parking lot.

"You saw Dina Langley today?" Eric asks.

I nod. "I also saw Brooks Wiley and Piper Peters."

While we walk, Eric phones in our dinner order to the pub. Then I tell him about my discussion with Dina and her revelation that Brooks and Jules offered her money to convince Claire's family to sell the *Familia* film rights.

"Even if Brooks and Jules convince Claire's family to sell the rights, it won't matter," Eric says.

"Why not?" I ask.

"Because Claire bequeathed *Familia* rights to Dina," he discloses. "Claire's family has no say whether they will make the books into movies."

We arrive back at Knitorious, and I stop at the back door while Eric unlocks it. "Why would Claire leave something that valuable to her assistant?" I ask, flabbergasted.

Eric shrugs and holds the door for Sophie and me. "I don't know," he replies. "But I don't think Dina knows yet that she's the beneficiary."

"Being the beneficiary might make her the next target," I say.

However, if she did know, it also gives her a motive to kill Claire.

CHAPTER 19

WHILE WE WAIT for dinner to arrive, we turn Eric's apartment upside down, looking for his laptop cord. He hoped it would be in his office at the station, but it's not.

"It's not here," I state the obvious, reassembling the sofa cushions.

"It's not anywhere," he grumbles.

"Did you check your car?"

He nods.

"My car?"

He nods.

"The store?

He holds up his index finger. "Not yet. But only because I never work in the store," he reasons, opening the door and thudding down the stairs.

"Bring my purse when you come back. I'll check it just in case," I call after him.

I doubt his cord is in my purse, but goodness knows I've found stranger things in there, so there's no harm in looking.

While Eric searches the store for his laptop cord, I put his apartment back together and feed Sophie her dinner.

Our food arrives while he's searching the store, so he comes back upstairs with dinner and my purse, but no laptop cord. I search my purse while he unboxes the food and sets the table.

"No cord," I say, shoving everything back inside.

"It's like it disappeared," he says. "I swear I left it at the house the other day when I was working from home doing budget stuff," he insists.

"I'll look again when I go home."

"No point," he says, "I searched the house so thoroughly you'd swear I had a warrant."

While I satisfy my craving for Irish nachos, and Eric digs into his steak and fries, I tell him about my discussion with Brooks Wiley and his reluctant admission that he and Jules are close.

"We'll have to take Brooks's word for it," Eric huffs. "I haven't questioned Jules. I can't get near her."

"Why?" I ask. "Just because she's famous doesn't mean she's above the law."

"No, but it means she can afford to surround herself with multiple layers of handlers and lawyers who won't let me access her." He cuts a piece of steak. "I can't even get her on the phone, which means I can't verify whether Brooks was with her when Claire was killed. Until I talk to her, Brooks's alibi is unverified." He shoves a piece of meat in his mouth.

I think about the business card Jules gave me, and her request for me to contact her after I passed along her gift to Claire.

"What if I talk to her," I suggest. "Jules will meet with me. Alone." I sound more confident than I am.

Eric looks dubious. "Without her entourage?"

I nod. "She was alone when she visited me the first time," I reason. "And if someone is with her, I'll refuse to talk to her unless we're alone."

"The situation has changed since Jules visited you on Wednesday," Eric reminds me. "With Claire dead and Jules knowing I want to talk to her, she might not come."

"Her goal hasn't changed," I counter. "She and Brooks are still trying to secure the film rights to *Familia*." Full, I slide the rest of my nachos toward him. "I can try, and if she doesn't come, we're no further behind. Nothing ventured, nothing gained, and all that."

"Even if she shows up, I can't question her." He pushes his empty plate aside and pulls my leftover nachos into its place. "In fact, don't even tell me. Plausible deniability. It's better if I don't know what you're up to. Jules Janssen lawyered up. Anything she says to me wouldn't be admissible because I'm a cop."

"Lucky for you, I'm not."

AFTER DINNER we watch an episode of our favourite home renovation reality show. By the time I get home, I'm physically spent from moving boxes of books, and mentally exhausted from trying to make sense of what we know so far about Claire's death. It's like trying to put together a puzzle that only has outside pieces—it doesn't make sense.

My dad and Zoe are already asleep, so I tread quietly through the house while I get ready for bed and put Sophie outside one last time before we turn in.

While Sophie is in the backyard doing her final perimeter check for the night, I walk through the house, gathering the dog toys she left scattered around the floor. I swear this corgi has enough toys for ten dogs. I'm about to drop the armload of squeaky, stuffy, bouncy toys into Sophie's toy box when I see it. Plain as day. Eric's laptop cord. Sitting in the bottom of the empty toy box. I must've gathered it up with Sophie's toys and dropped in there by accident. I unload the toys I'm carrying into the box and pull out the laptop cord. I snap a picture of the cord with my cell phone and text it to Eric.

Me: Look what I found!
Eric: OMG! Where was it?
Me: Sophie's toy box.
Eric: The one place I didn't look.
Me: Want me to drop it off?

Eric: Stay there. I'll pick it up. I'll be there in 10 minutes.

Me: Text me from the driveway so Sophie doesn't bark and wake up Dad and Zoe.

Eric: K.

Sure enough, ten minutes later, Eric texts to let me know he's outside. I slip on the fuzzy slides I wear for excursions into the garage, grab the laptop cord, and silently close the front door behind me.

"Sorry," I say, hopping into the passenger seat of his car and lunging the cord at him.

"Sorry for what, babe? You found it!"

"I suspect I might also be the one who lost it," I explain, telling him how I probably scooped up the cord with Sophie's toys and deposited it in her toy box.

"Actually, I think it was me. On Thursday morning, when we expected your dad and Zoe to arrive before dinner…"

While Eric and I argue over who was the last person to clean up Sophie's toys and lose the stupid laptop cord, his phone dings.

"Phillip," Eric says.

Phillip is my next-door neighbour at home and at work. I glance over Eric's shoulder, and it doesn't look like Phillip is home; his house is dark, and his floral-wrapped delivery van isn't in the driveway.

"Is everything OK?" I ask.

It's late for Phillip to be texting without a reason. He

gets up horribly early most mornings to receive deliveries at his florist shop.

"There's someone in the store," Eric replies, typing a response.

"Wilde Flowers?" I ask, assuming he's referring to Phillip's store.

Eric shakes his head. "Knitorious."

"What?!"

"You should wait here," he suggests, tossing the laptop cord in the backseat and starting the car.

I close the car door and buckle my seatbelt. "No way."

"Babe, you're wearing dragonfly jammies and fuzzy slides."

"Drive," I insist, unwilling to argue. "Or I can drive myself and meet you there."

On the short drive to Knitorious, Eric summons backup and reminds me three times to wait in the car.

He parks in the farthest parking spot and turns off the ignition.

"Wait. In. The. Car." He tries to look stern, but it doesn't suit him.

"Be careful," I say. "Maybe you should wait for backup."

"They're already here," Eric informs me. I look around. Nothing but bushes, darkness, and Phillip's floral-wrapped delivery van. "It's probably a false alarm anyway," he says, trying to ease my worry. "Phillip said he saw someone using a flashlight, but it could've been a head light reflecting off the display window," he reasons. "I'll be right back. I love you." He kisses me then exits the car, closing the door silently behind him.

A tap on the rear passenger-side window makes me almost jump out of my skin. Phillip is squatting next to the car and tapping the window with a key. I push the button on the armrest and unlock the door.

"Geez, Phillip, you scared the life out of me!" I say when he crawls into the backseat.

"Sorry, Megan!" he hisses. "I was hiding in my van," he explains in hushed tones. "There's someone in your store. I heard them through the wall. I didn't see your or Eric's car in the parking lot, and I worried it might be a critter. I looked through the front window and saw a silhouette. They were carrying a flashlight."

"Were they near the cash register?" I ask.

If I were going to rob a store, I wouldn't choose a yarn store. We have hardly any cash. We do a lot of sales online, and most of our in-store sales are debit or credit.

"No," he replies. "They were near the back room."

Maybe they're stealing yarn? What other reason could someone have for breaking into a yarn store?

"Did you get your April bouquet?" Phillips whispers. "I left it with Connie and Zoe yesterday."

"Yes," I reply. "Thank you. It's gorgeous, Phillip."

"Well, I got the most beautiful delivery of cherry blossoms. I know they're one of your favourites, and I thought they might add to the ambience at your dad's book signing..."

While Phillip and I discuss April flowers, I contemplate how absurd this is; we're out here talking about seasonal blooms while the love of my life is potentially taking down a dangerous intruder less than a hundred metres away. My phone dings, making Phillip and I gasp and jump.

Eric: Suspect apprehended! You can come inside.

Between the car and the store, Phillip and I ponder whether the intruder is someone we know, and why they broke into Knitorious. We can't remember the last time a local business was robbed. We're locked arm-in-arm and cling to each other for dear life.

I open the back door, and a uniformed officer stands aside so Philip and I can enter the store together, like conjoined twins, because I'm not letting go of him, and he's not letting go of me.

Three uniformed officers crowd the back room, plus Eric. One of the uniformed officers stands aside to reveal the intruder, cuffed and sitting on the stairs that lead to the apartment.

CHAPTER 20

"Piper Peters!" I gasp and bring my hand to my mouth.

Phillip inhales sharply. "Piper!" he wheezes, sounding dramatic and horrified. Then he whispers in my ear, "Do we know her?"

"Yes." I nod. "We know her."

An officer approaches us and asks Phillip to go with him to provide a statement.

"Will you be OK without me?" Phillip asks.

"I think so." I nod, unable to take my eyes off Piper. "How about you?" I ask. "Will you be OK?"

"You'll know if I'm not," he says, prying our arms apart. "I'll scream your name so loud they'll hear me on the other side of the lake."

"I'll be right here, Phillip." I throw my arms around him. "Thank you!"

Piper isn't wearing her authentic Victorian-era

mourning attire. She's wearing black leggings, black running shoes with black soles, and a black hoodie. A black backpack rests nearby. She looks like a cat burglar. She wasn't kidding when she said she packs an outfit for every contingency.

"Nice PJs," Piper says, smiling. "I love dragonflies." She greets me like we've bumped into each other under normal circumstances.

"Piper, what are you doing here?" I demand.

"Stealing Claire's books," she explains as though it were a foregone conclusion.

"What books?" I screw up my face in confusion and look back and forth between her and Eric.

"The signed books you helped Dina remove from the rental cottage," Piper explains calmly. "I was told they would be here. But it appears I was misinformed."

This explains Piper's preoccupation with the back room at the book signing today, and yesterday when she was here to purchase the felted items. She was casing the joint.

"Who told you that?" I ask, already knowing the answer.

"I'm afraid I'm not at liberty to say," she coos in her posh British accent.

"We asked her," Eric interjects. "She won't tell us either."

"I already know who told her," I inform him. "I just want to hear her say it." Piper extends her bottom lip out and blows a stray lock of hair from her face and rolls her eyes like a sulky teenager. "Why did Brooks Wiley tell you where to find Claire's signed books?" I inquire.

"I'm sorry, I don't know to whom you're referring," Piper insists, looking at her feet and feigning ignorance.

"How do you know it was Brooks?" Eric asks.

"Because when Brooks and Dina discussed where to move the books, I offered to store them here"—I gesture to the nearby storeroom—"but when Dina and I came here to drop them off, Zoe convinced us they'd be safer at chez Martel, so we took them there instead. Dina couldn't reach Brooks to clear it with him, but assured me she'd contact him and let him know about the last-minute location change. I guess she forgot."

"How were you planning to move the books?" Eric asks Piper. "There aren't any vehicles in the parking lot."

Good observation, Eric!

"Upon locating the books, I would contact my partner in crime, at which time he would arrive with a vehicle to transport them to an undisclosed location."

"Where's the undisclosed location?" I ask.

"I don't know," Piper admits. "He didn't disclose it to me."

I sigh. "How did she get in?" I ask Eric.

"She busted the lock," he replies, fanning the door to show me the damaged hardware.

"Where is Brooks now?" I ask, glaring at Piper.

Piper shrugs. "I've no idea," she replies.

"I think she's telling the truth," Eric says. "Piper, what were you and Brooks planning to do with the books?"

"I planned to preserve my half," she explains, "for posterity."

"You and Brooks planned to split the books?" I clarify. "He would keep half of them and you would keep half of them?"

"That's right," Piper confirms. "They've increased in value, you see. Because they are the last books Claire will ever sign. Brooks said he planned to capitalize on their value. Strike while the iron is hot, is how he said it, if I recall. He lined up buyers on an online forum for collectors. I have no interest in profiting from Claire's death, I just want to preserve the books for future generations."

Have the books increased so much that Brooks decided it would be worthwhile to kill Claire so he could sell them? Did Brooks and Piper conspire to kill Claire together? Or did they join forces just to steal the books? Why would Brooks want a partner to steal the books, anyway? If he stole them alone, he could've sold all of them instead of half. But this way Piper gets caught in the act instead of him. I think Brooks Wiley doesn't like to get his hands dirty. Or maybe Brooks had no intention of giving Piper half the books; that would explain why he didn't tell her where the undisclosed location is. Maybe after Piper stole the books and served her purpose, Brooks was planning to kill her too.

A uniformed officer stands guard over Piper while Eric and I walk through the store, making sure nothing is missing. Everything seems to be where I left it.

"We checked her backpack and there's nothing from the store in there. Just a burner phone, a small amount of cash, and the tools she used to break the lock on the back door," Eric says.

A burner phone is a phone purchased with cash. It doesn't have a monthly plan and can't be traced to an owner.

"Do we need to check the apartment?" I ask Eric when we re-enter the back room.

"Oh, I hardly touched anything in the upstairs flat," Piper interjects, giggling. "I'm not one for nosing through people's belongings," says the woman who broke into my store and touched everything.

"What do you mean you *hardly* touched anything?" Eric asks.

Piper shrugs. "I looked around. There were no books, so I left. There was no point in rifling through your drawers and cupboards." She giggles. "It's not like you could hide boxes of books in your underwear drawer." Then she becomes serious again. "Mind you, I relocated your Spathiphyllum wallisii."

"You relocated his *what*?" I ask, wondering what the heck she's talking about.

"His peace lily," she clarifies. "It was on the windowsill. They prefer indirect sunlight, so I moved it to the coffee table. And I watered it." She looks at Eric with a serious expression on her face. "The soil was dry to the touch. You must keep the soil moist," she scolds.

She's crazy. There's no other explanation. If she's not crazy, she deserves an Academy Award.

While Eric goes upstairs to make sure nothing is missing or damaged in the apartment, Phillip informs me he's finished giving his statement, and he's going home. I thank him again for having my back. We're hugging when Piper's backpack rings.

"Brooks!" I say to the uniformed officer who's guarding Piper. "It must be him."

I bet he's calling to find out why Piper hasn't contacted him yet.

"Chief!" the officer yells.

Eric's feet thump down the stairs as the uniformed officer unzips the backpack and holds it open toward him. Eric pulls the phone out of the laptop with his gloved hand and raises the index finger of his other hand to his lips in a *shhh* motion. We all nod in acknowledgement.

Eric accepts the call and holds the phone to Piper's ear, but she says nothing. He raises his eyebrows and nods at her, as if willing her to speak. Piper purses her lips and turns away from the phone, refusing to answer the call. He puts the phone near his ear.

"Brooks Wiley. I know it's you. This is Eric Sloane from the Harmony Lake Police Department. We know everything." He pauses, but I don't think Brooks speaks. "Let's do this the easy way. Tell me where you are." Eric pulls the phone away from his ear. "He hung up."

The collective sigh in the back room sounds like a deflating balloon.

Eric instructs the first uniformed officer to accompany Phillip to his van, then check on Dina Langley, and stand guard outside her hotel room. They leave.

He instructs the second officer to take Piper to the police station and lists various charges to file against her. The officer leads Piper away by the arm.

The third officer's instructions are to go to chez Martel and stand guard over the books and the occupants of the house. The officer leaves.

"The occupants of the house?" I ask with a lump in my throat and my heart pounding in my ears. "Do you think Dad and Zoe are in danger?"

"No, I'm sure they're fine. I'm being extra cautious. The books are there, and Brooks wants them. I don't think he'd be dumb enough to show up there, though," Eric assures me. "But if it's all right with you, I'll stay over tonight." Despite his reassuring words, Eric is worried enough to break his self-imposed rule about not having sleepovers while my dad is in town.

He makes a phone call and dispatches officers to King of the Hill to check if Brooks is in his hotel room. He also orders a BOLO for Brooks and his car.

BOLO is cop speak for Be On The Lookout. Officers will keep an eye out for Brooks and take him into custody if he surfaces.

"I want to go home," I say.

Eric nods. "We'll leave through the front door," he says, sliding the barrel bolt—the only remaining functional lock—into the locked position on the inside of the back door.

His phone dings, rings, and vibrates non-stop on the short drive home, but he doesn't check it because he's driving.

As soon as he turns off the engine, Eric checks his phone.

"Brooks isn't in his hotel room," he advises me. "His things are still there, including his passport, so he hasn't gone far."

"What about Dina?" I ask.

"Dina's fine," Eric replies. "The last time she spoke to Brooks was yesterday. She told the officer she'll notify us right away if Brooks contacts her."

Brooks's unknown whereabouts is like finding a spider on the ceiling. The situation is tenable as long as you know where the spider is, but if you look up and the spider isn't there, you panic, wondering where it went and if it's closer to you than you'd like.

CHAPTER 21

MONDAY, April 19th

"Good morning, Dad!" I summon a chipper voice and a smile, hoping to hide my exhaustion after tossing and turning all night.

"Good morning, Bean!" He smiles at me over his newspaper and reading glasses.

"Did you walk to the store this morning to get a paper?" I ask, wondering if the officer parked at the bottom of the driveway stopped him.

"I tried," my dad replies, closing the paper and laying it on his lap. "But Eric asked me to stay here. He dispatched the officer who's guarding the house to get a newspaper for me."

"Where is Eric?" I ask, dropping a coffee pod into the coffeemaker.

"Running," my dad replies. "He said we'd talk about it when you wake up."

I nod and open the back door for Sophie. "Do you want to wait until Zoe wakes up?"

He shakes his head. "I'll catch her up later."

While Sophie eats breakfast, and I sip my coffee, I tell my dad everything that went down last night and explain why Eric deemed it necessary to post a patrol car outside the house.

"He's being extra cautious until Brooks is in police custody," I say in conclusion.

"Hang on," my dad says, then reaches for the notebook and pen on the table next to his armchair. "I want to take notes. I can use some of this in my book."

"Well, I'm glad we can help with your research," I half-joke as I get up to put my empty mug in the dishwasher.

I pick up my phone for the first time today, and scroll through the myriad of unread messages. Most from friends and neighbours wanting to know what happened last night, and why there's a patrol car outside the house.

First, I respond to Connie and April so our nearest and dearest will know we're OK.

Next, I text Ryan, Harmony Lake's resident handyperson, and ask him to stop by Knitorious to fix the broken lock. He replies, saying he'll meet me at the store later this morning.

Last but not least, I text Jules Janssen and ask her if she wants to know what Claire said about her gift on Wednesday. Jules Janssen isn't quick to respond.

While I'm busy reading and responding to texts, Eric comes home from his run.

"Was there a Brooks Wiley sighting overnight?" I ask, hoping Brooks is in custody, and we'll finally get some answers about Claire's murder.

Eric shakes his head. "Nothing." He kisses me good morning, and I scrunch my nose at his post-run muskiness. "Wait for me. I want to drive you to work." It's a statement, not a suggestion or a question. He's in bodyguard mode.

"OK." I nod.

I feel safe going to the store on my own, but I'm too tired to argue.

He gets in the shower, and Zoe wakes up, so my dad and I update her on everything that happened while she slept.

KNITORIOUS ISN'T OPEN on Mondays, but I need to finish flattening and recycling the empty boxes from the book signing, and re-shelve the yarn we removed from the store to accommodate my dad's books. Also, I need to be there when Ryan fixes the back door.

When we arrive at Knitorious, there is a courier truck in the parking lot. A man wearing a courier company uniform waits by the back door. He's leaning against a hand truck.

"The books!" I exclaim, smacking my palm against

my forehead. "Claire's publisher sent him to pick up the signed books. With all the kerfuffle over the past couple of days, I forgot."

"I'll take care of it," Eric offers. "I'll meet you inside."

As I walk around the corner to the front door, Eric squints into the morning sun and tells the driver there's a misunderstanding about the location of the books.

As soon as I'm inside the store, I call my dad and Zoe to give them a heads up about the courier's imminent arrival at chez Martel.

"Don't worry, Bean!" my dad assures me. "Eric sent a text, and the officer stationed outside is here with us. We'll be sure the courier picks them up."

I can't wait for those books to leave Harmony Lake. It will be a relief not to worry about anyone breaking into my house to steal them.

As soon as we end the call, my phone rings.

"Is everything OK in there?" Eric asks.

"It's all good," I reply. "Don't worry."

"OK. I'll see you in a few minutes."

He sounds distracted; he must've run into someone or got caught up talking to the courier.

I drop my cell phone in my purse and toss it onto the counter. Hands on hips, I exhale loudly and survey the store, deciding where to start.

"Megan, don't scream."

A scream escapes me, but I cover my mouth with both hands and stifle it.

"How did you get in?" I ask, wide-eyed and mortified.

"I picked the lock," he replies in his melodious creole accent.

He points at the front door. If he can pick this lock, he could've picked the lock to the den at Claire's rental cottage.

"What are you doing here, Brooks?"

He's standing in the doorway between the back room and the store.

"I want to explain myself," he says, his hands in front of him as if he's not a threat.

"Explain why you killed Claire Rivera?" I ask.

Brooks shakes his head. "I did not kill Claire."

He sounds adamant, but I remind myself he's a skilled liar.

"Why should I believe you?" I ask. "You lied about your relationship with Jules. You lied about being in your hotel room when Claire was murdered, and you lied about your relationship with Piper Peters."

Where's Eric? He can't still be talking to the courier.

"First," he raises his index finger. "The only thing I lied about is my relationship with Jules," he insists. "I lied to protect her privacy. Do you know how hard it is for her to avoid the tabloids?"

"Do I care?" My voice is thick with sarcasm.

"I didn't lie about my alibi," he continues. "I told your boyfriend I was at the hotel when Claire was murdered. I didn't say I was in my room."

A lie by omission is a lie, nonetheless.

"You were in Jules's room?" I presume.

He nods. "That's right. Ask her entourage, lots of them saw me."

"Jules and her people aren't cooperating with the police," I advise him. "Didn't she tell you? They lawyered up. As far as the police are concerned, you don't have an alibi." Brooks curses under his breath, and the muscles in his jaw clench and unclench.

"I didn't lie about Piper, either," he tells me. "She is crazy. Like a fox. I think she killed Claire because it upset her when Claire announced she was ending the Familia series. Those aren't just books to Piper, they're real. That's why she broke into your shop to help me get them. She's built her life around them."

"So have you. Claire was your biggest client and your biggest source of income," I point out. "Trying to recruit Mitchell Monroe to fill the empty spot on your client list the day after Claire's murder doesn't look good for you."

Now would be a great time to show up, Eric!

"I would have pitched my services to Mitchell whether Claire was dead or alive," he says, shaking his head and sitting at the harvest table. "It's all about the money. That's why I wanted the books. With Claire gone, my income from her will dry up. I panicked and thought I could sell the signed books for a good price to fill in the gap." He looks at me with pleading eyes. "Think about it, Megan," he taps his bald head with his finger. "Why would I kill Claire? She was my meal ticket."

I shift my weight from one foot to the other, but stay put, planted within arm's reach of the front door.

"Because she refused to sell the film rights," I speculate. "The film rights would earn you millions of dollars. That's why you approached her family to sell them less than two days after Claire's murder."

I wish Eric would hurry.

"The only reason I approached Claire's family is because Dina convinced me it was a good idea," he says, sounding desperate. "She told me Claire's family wanted to sell the rights. She told me they were huge Jules Janssen fans, and she even suggested that if Jules was part of the sales pitch, it would help to convince them."

That doesn't sound like Dina. It doesn't vibe with what Dina told me, and her story has been way more consistent than Brooks's story.

"Why should I believe you?" I ask.

"Because it's the truth." He smacks the tabletop with his open palm, and I take a step backward, toward the door. Brooks takes a deep breath and blows it out. "I might be shady, but I'm not a killer."

"Why did you tell Jules where Claire and Dina were staying in Harmony Lake? You know they wanted their location to remain private."

He shrugs. "Because she asked me. And I love Jules. I'd do anything for her."

Would he commit murder for her?

"Brooks," I say, trying to sound as composed as possible, "you need to tell your story to the police…"

"No way." He stands up, shaking his head. "They won't believe me. They're looking for evidence to charge me, not clear me." He backs away from the harvest table, toward the back room. "I've been here too long." He glances behind him, then looks back at me. "I have to go." He turns, and moments later, the back door slams shut.

I lunge toward the counter and grab my phone from my purse. I run toward the back door. Maybe I can tell which direction Brooks went. I throw open the door and run into the parking lot.

He's gone. There's no sign of him. The parking lot is empty except for Phillip's delivery van and Eric's car.

Where's Eric? Did he run after Brooks? Should I call 9-1-1? I turn my head in every direction, searching for a sign of either man.

"Megan?" His voice is distant. It's coming from inside the store. "Babe?" I turn toward the back door. Eric appears in the doorway. "What are you doing? Are you OK?" He's next to me now, turning his head. Scanning the parking lot. Searching with me, but he doesn't know what we're searching for.

"Brooks was here. I don't know where he went." I look up at him. "He's gone. I tried to keep him here as long as I could. I'm sorry."

"Are you OK?" He grips my shoulders and looks me up and down. "Did he touch you?"

I shake my head. "I'm fine. He stayed away from me."

Eric turns me around and guides me inside. I sink into the sofa in the cozy sitting area, and he hands me a coffee. Maple pecan latte. He went to get me a coffee.

"Thank you." I force a small smile.

"This is my fault, babe. I'm so sorry." He looks like he might cry.

"It's not your fault. Brooks's actions are Brooks's fault and no one else." I shake my head. "You did nothing wrong. Anyway, no one was hurt."

"I should've come inside ahead of you and cleared the store... rookie mistake," he says, shaking his head. "The courier could've waited." He sounds angry. His thumbs move at lightning speed across the keyboard on his phone. "Everyone is looking for Brooks. When I get hold of him..." His voice trails off at the end of his sentence.

"He had no intention of hurting me," I assure him. "Why would he? I haven't done anything to him."

Eric sits next to me and pulls me into him. I rest my head on his chest and take a deep breath. He smells like a forest after it rains and the sun comes out. It's my favourite smell. He kisses the top of my head. He tells me he loves me and apologizes again. His guilt is palpable. His chin rests on the top of my head.

"We're getting a security system for the store," he says, like it's a done deal.

"We are?" I ask.

I don't think we need a security system at Knitorious, but now isn't the time to argue, so I swallow the urge to disagree with him.

I feel him nod. "We'll get the same system as the house." He squeezes me. "Two intruders are too many." He shakes his head. "This won't happen again. When I think about what could've happened..." He swallows hard. His hand clenches into a fist, then relaxes. "You're here fending off a dangerous fugitive while I was standing in line buying coffee..." His voice hitches on the last word of his incomplete sentence, and he squeezes me again.

"I didn't fend off anyone. Nothing happened," I remind him. "Everyone is fine."

"Do you need to look for him?" I ask, sitting up to sip my coffee.

"Every cop on the force is looking for Brooks Wiley," Eric reminds me, tucking a stray curl behind my ear. "How did he get in here?"

"He says he picked the lock." I point to the front door.

"If he could pick this lock, he could've picked the lock on the den at Claire's rental cottage," Eric points out, coming to my previous conclusion. "What did he want? Was he looking for the books?"

"I don't know if he was looking for the books," I reply. "He said he wanted to explain himself."

"Did he?"

I nod, then tell Eric about my conversation with Brooks.

"Do you believe him?" Eric asks at the end of my account.

"Which part?" I ask. "I feel like lying comes easy to Brooks, you know?"

Eric nods. "I'm familiar with the type."

"He makes a good point, though, about how killing Claire would kill most of his income. It wouldn't be a smart move, and while Brooks might be an accomplished liar, he strikes me as a smart person. Too smart to kill his biggest source of income."

"But she wouldn't be his biggest source of income if she stopped writing," Eric points out. "And Jules has a lot more money than Claire. Maybe now that he's with Jules, he decided Claire was expendable."

I startle at the sound of three sharp raps on the door. Heavy shoulders, long arms, I remind myself, letting out a deep breath.

"It's probably Ryan," I say to Eric as he stands up to answer the door. My phone dings, and I glance at it. "Eric! Stop!"

He stops, and I tilt my phone so he can see it.

Jules: Are you there? The door is locked.

Eric blurts out a curse word. "I can't be here when you talk to her."

"Just a sec," I tell him as I type a response to Jules's text.

Me: I'll be right there. Give me two minutes.

"Leave through the back door." I jerk my head toward the back of the store.

"I'm not leaving!" He sounds offended. "What if Brooks comes back?"

"He won't," I insist, despite having no idea what Brooks Wiley's intentions are. "I'll text you as soon as Jules leaves. I'll be fine. Ryan will be here soon, and if I scream, Phillip will hear me through the wall." I nudge him toward the back of the store. "Just go. If you don't go, I can't talk to her."

With a frustrated groan, Eric disappears into the back room. I plaster a cheerful smile on my face and open the door.

CHAPTER 22

"Hɪ, Jᴜʟᴇs!"

"Thanks for reaching out," she says, leaning in for an awkward side-hug where we touch each other's shoulders and kind of lean into one another. "You have good timing. I'm leaving town tonight."

She steps inside and watches me lock the door.

"We're closed on Mondays," I explain. "I came in today to clean up. The store is in shambles after the book signing. Can I get you a coffee, or tea, or anything?"

"No, thank you." Her smile displays a tremendous number of teeth. "I'm fine."

"Speaking of book signings, I hear yours went very well on Saturday."

"Yes, it was a huge success," Jules responds, taking off her sunglasses and laying her backpack on the floor at her feet.

While Jules gives me the highlights of her book signing, I join her in the cozy sitting area with my maple pecan latte. Just like the first time we met, Jules is incognito today. She's wearing a pair of leggings—the athletic kind you'd wear for running—a pink tank top with a pink running jacket zipped up halfway, and black running shoes. Her auburn hair is tucked into her black baseball cap with the bill pulled down to shield her face. She looks like any other yummy mummy running errands after dropping off the kids at school.

"Did Brooks Wiley come to your signing and get you to sign a book for him?" I ask.

A panicked micro-expression flashes across Jules's face.

"Who?"

I can see why she earned an academy award.

"Tall guy... handsome... expensive Italian suits... face that looks like it was sculpted by a Greek god... bald... sultry accent?"

She shakes her head. "Doesn't ring a bell," she says, "but if he looks anything like you describe him, I *wish* I knew him." We laugh.

"Weird," I comment. "I'm sure I saw you making out with him in the alley beside the store on Wednesday." I reach for my phone on the coffee table. "In fact, I think I have a photo of you kissing with his hand on your backside."

"Let's cut the crap, Megan," Jules says, her tone

business-like. "Fine. I know Brooks." She points to my phone. "Delete the photo."

"There is no photo," I admit. "I wanted to see how far you'd take the lie."

She's not amused. Even her exhale sounds annoyed.

"I go to great lengths to protect my privacy," she explains.

"It's too bad you don't go to the same lengths to protect other people's privacy," I counter.

She narrows her eyes. "What is that supposed to mean?" she asks, defensive.

"It means you gave Piper Peters the address and directions to Claire Rivera's rental cottage." Jules's face softens, and her shoulders slump. "Why would you do that? Brooks told you Piper was unstable and had a history of threatening Claire."

"Look, it wasn't my finest moment," Jules admits. "I knew about Claire's trouble with Piper. Brooks told me about the disturbing letters and emails Piper sent. I empathize. I've dealt with more than my fair share of obsessed fans. A few months ago, when Brooks told me Piper showed up on Claire's doorstep, I reached out to offer Claire support."

"Moral support?" I ask.

Jules shrugs one shoulder. "Yes, and other support. I have a first-rate security team and legal advisers. They deal with fans like Piper Peters on the regular. I offered Claire their services. Free. No strings attached."

"Did Claire accept your generous offer?"

She shakes her head. "She didn't even respond to my offer. Brooks said Claire thought that if she accepted my offer, I'd use it as leverage to pressure her into selling me the *Familia* movie rights."

"That doesn't explain why you disclosed Claire's location to Piper."

"It made sense at the time. It was a spur-of-the-moment decision," she justifies. "I saw Piper waiting in line, and the idea jumped into my head. I acted without thinking it through," Jules explains, sitting up a little straighter. "Claire wouldn't talk to me at all. She wouldn't reply to emails, accept phone calls, or even meet with my representatives. I thought if Piper showed up on her doorstep in Harmony Lake, it would frighten Claire enough to contact me and take me up on my offer to help her."

"And the line of communication between you and Claire would be open," I conclude.

"That was my plan."

"That was a dangerous plan, Jules," I say, shaking my head. "What if Piper used the information you gave her to kill Claire?"

"I know." Jules raises her hand in a stop motion. "I realized it was a horrible idea as soon as I did it. I regretted it immediately."

"But you didn't regret it enough to warn Claire that Piper knew her location?"

"It never occurred to me that anyone would die!"

"Where were you when Claire was murdered?" I ask without warning so I can gauge her response.

"I was busy," Jules replies, shrugging one shoulder. "I'm always busy."

"Can you be more specific?" I urge. "If the police can account for your whereabouts, they'll eliminate you as a suspect and leave you alone."

"Let's see." Her gaze shifts to the right, like she's trying to remember something. "Thursday morning, I had a call with New York about an upcoming project." She drums her meticulously manicured fingers on her lap. "Then I went swimming in the hotel pool." She looks at me. "The hotel manager closed the pool just for me."

"Did anyone swim with you?"

"No," Jules replies.

"What time did you finish swimming?" I ask.

"Lunchtime," she replies. "I went back to my room, showered, and got dressed. I ordered soup and salad from room service. My manager sat with me while I ate, and we went over my schedule for the New York project. After lunch, I had a massage and a facial." She smiles.

"At a local salon?"

Jules laughs. "No. I have my own people. They do everything for me. I received the spa treatments in my hotel room."

"You didn't mention Brooks. Was he with you on Thursday?"

She presses her lips into a thin line and shakes her head. "I didn't see Brooks until Thursday evening."

"Brooks says he was in your room all day on Thursday, starting from late morning."

"Which room?" she asks.

"How many rooms do you have?"

"The entire top floor of the hotel," she replies as if it should be obvious. "I need a lot of rooms, Megan." She counts on her fingers. "A room for me, a room for my manager, rooms for my security team, rooms for my glam squad, a room for my publicist, a room for my agent…."

I raise my hand in a stop motion. "I get it. You have an entourage."

"He could've been there, and I just didn't see him," she surmises. "But if he was there, someone saw him. My team is pretty busy. Lots of comings and goings."

"Jules, you need to let your team talk to the police. Unless someone says they saw Brooks at the time of Claire's murder, he'll stay on the suspect list. He needs your help."

"It's not up to me," she explains. "It's up to the lawyers."

"The lawyers work for you," I remind her. "If you tell them you want to cooperate with the police, they'll listen to you. Don't you want to help Brooks? He's on the run. He's practically a fugitive, and he's making poor decisions."

"Is that why he's not returning my texts?" she asks.

I get the sense Jules Janssen isn't very concerned about her boyfriend's legal problems. At all. It's like he's just another member of her entourage.

"Jules, he lied about his alibi to protect your privacy. He loves you."

"Lots of people love me." She shrugs.

"But I think Brooks believes you feel the same about him."

"He's so sweet." She tilts her ear toward her shoulder and smiles. "Brooks knows our situationship is casual."

"Situationship?" I ask.

"An undefined relationship situation," she explains. "Hanging out with Brooks is fun. And lord knows, he's hot." She fans her hand in front of her face. "We bonded over the common goal of making *Familia* into a movie, but I'm not looking for anything permanent. I made it crystal clear to him. If Brooks caught feelings for me, that's his problem. I warned him."

Sounds cold. I almost pity Brooks. Maybe he killed Claire to make Jules love him. Maybe, he thought with Claire out of the way, he'd be able to secure the film rights, and Jules would fall head over heels for him. Was Claire's murder Brooks's attempt to be Jules's knight in shining armour?

"Do you think Brooks loves you enough to kill for you?" I ask quietly.

Jules shrugs. "How would I know? I didn't ask him to kill anyone for me." Jules pulls her phone out of her jacket pocket and checks the time. "I have to get going." She stands up and grabs her backpack. "You didn't reach out to me to tell me what Claire said about the gift, did you?"

"It was my secondary reason," I admit. "She accepted the gift, but said she'd only give up the film rights over her dead body."

"Creepy," Jules remarks with a shudder.

Before she leaves, Jules agrees to give me the names and phone numbers of the people from New York who she spoke with on Thursday morning. I open my planner to a blank note page and hand her a pen. Using her phone for reference, she jots down five names and phone numbers.

"And I'll talk to my lawyers and ask them to be more cooperative with your local police," she says.

"Thanks," I reply. "One more thing," I say before I unlock the door. "At your book signing on Saturday, you told the mayor you were confident you'd acquire the film rights to *Familia* because you just eliminated a major obstacle. What did you mean? Were you referring to Claire?"

"No," she replies, laughing. "Of course not. On Saturday morning, I secured one of the best directors in the industry. I won't tell you his name, but I guarantee you've seen lots of his movies. He'll impress whoever ends up owning the *Familia* rights." I unlock the door. "That's all I meant." She waves. "Bye, Megan."

"Bye, Jules. Safe travels."

I take a picture of the names and numbers Jules wrote in my planner and text them to Eric. He asks me how our visit went and whether I learned anything that might help solve Claire's murder.

To be honest, I don't know.

Was Jules honest with me about everything she said, or was she acting? If she can sneak around town incognito to visit me, make out with Brooks, and talk to Piper without being recognized, she could easily go to Claire's rental cottage with no one noticing. And I'm sure Jules's team will verify her alibi; their livelihoods depend on it.

Other than Jules agreeing to let her entourage cooperate with the police, our conversation didn't rule out or further incriminate any of the suspects. Who killed Claire, and why, is still as clear as mud.

CHAPTER 23

CHAPTER 23

APRIL: *The bakery is DEAD today. I'm sooo bored!*

Me: *As soon as I finish here, I'll come visit you!*

April: *Yay! I want to hear about everything that happened last night.*

Me: *Want me to call you? We can talk while I re-shelve the yarn.*

April: *I can't talk right now. Guess who is here again?*

Me: *Give me a hint.*

April: *She's blonde, bubbly, and loves lemon meringue tarts.*

Me: *Dina Langley?*

April: *Yup! She's been here all morning. Just her and me. All alone.*

Me: *Where's T?*

April: *She drove to Harmony Hills to load up on baking supplies. She'll be back later.*

Me: I hope Dina hangs around until I get there. I want to ask her about some things Brooks said.

I just flattened the last box, and now I'm tying all the flattened boxes together with twine so they'll be easier to drag to the curb on recycling day.

Two sharp raps on the back door startle me, and I almost cut myself with the utility knife. I'll be less jumpy when Claire's murderer is off the streets.

"Who is it?" I shout through the locked door.

"It's just me, Megan."

"Hi, Ryan," I say with a smile when I open the door. "Thanks for fitting me in. I know it's last minute."

"*Pshaw.*" He flicks away my comment with his hand. "That's what family is for."

Ryan and I aren't family in the biological sense of the word. Or in the related-by-marriage sense of the word. Ryan's dad is Archie. Archie is Connie's partner. Connie is my surrogate mum. According to Ryan, this makes us stepsiblings. Ryan is part of my modern, non-traditional family.

"*Phwoooooh,*" Ryan whistles. "She sure did a number on this lock."

"Can you fix it?" I ask.

"Let me take a closer look," he replies, squatting and putting his face up to the broken mechanism. "If I have to replace it, I have locks in my truck. Either way, you'll have a functional lock when I leave."

"Thank you," I say. "It's a weight off my mind."

While Ryan works his magic on the back door, I walk to and from the back room, carrying skeins of yarn from the storage closet to the store. When he's finished fixing the lock and announces he's leaving, I've already re-shelved all the bulky, Aran, and worsted weight yarns.

I'M CHALLENGING myself to carry the last of the lace weight yarn in one armload when someone taps three times on the front door. It's busier here than at Grand Central Station. The knocking is followed by intense scratching; whoever it is has Sophie with them.

"Just a sec!" I holler from near the lace weight yarn shelves.

I dump the lace weight yarn into the shelves, creating yarn chaos, and jog to the front door.

"Hi, Dad!" We kiss cheeks. "Hi, Soph!" She puts her front paws on my knees, and I rub her. I stand aside so they can come in. "Where's Zoe?"

"Grocery shopping. She said to tell you not to worry about dinner tonight, she wants to cook."

"That's nice of her," I say. "Sometimes I wish you guys lived closer."

"So we can cook for you?" he asks, laughing.

"It would be a nice perk," I reply. "But it would be nice to see you more often."

"Even if we lived up the street, you wouldn't see

much more of us," he reminds me. "We travel most of the year."

"I know." I sigh. "What brings you and Sophie into town?"

"It was time for Sophie's midday walk, and I thought she could stay here while I take one of my favourite daughters out for lunch."

"I'd love that," I say, smiling.

"Can we go in a few minutes?" I ask. "I want to finish shelving this yarn."

I return to the yarn I shoved into the lace weight shelves and sort it by colour and brand as fast as I can.

"Ouch!"

"Dad, are you OK?" I ask from the back of the store where I'm finding shelf space for a few rogue skeins of yarn.

"Mmm-hmm," he replies with the tip of his index finger in his mouth.

I grab the first-aid kit and rush to his side.

"What happened?" I open the first aid box.

"I pricked my finger with that thing." He points to my felting needle. It's on the end table in the cozy sitting area, next to my almost-finished Sophie figurine.

"How?" I ask, using a piece of gauze to apply direct pressure to his wound.

"I just picked it up to look at it," he explains. "I was curious. It doesn't look as sharp as it feels!"

Tearing open an alcohol wipe, I explain the tool has small barbs near the end that make it sharper than it looks. He winces when the alcohol touches his finger.

"It hurts more when you pull it out than it does when it goes in," I explain.

"That Dina lady who came to the book signing yesterday had one floating around in her backpack, so I assumed it must not be very sharp," he says.

"Dina?" I ask. "The young woman who brought all the *Shark Attack* books with her?"

Dad nods. "That's right. Claire Rivera's assistant."

This must be what they laughed about when he signed Dina's books and made the comment about keeping pickpockets out of her backpack. But Dina told me she isn't a needle felter, so why would she carry a needle? And if she is a felter, why would she lie about it? It's hardly a controversial hobby; there's no reason to be a closet felter and keep her needle felting habit a secret.

"What else did you see in Dina's backpack?" I ask.

"I only had a quick peek when she pulled out the books," Dad replies. "The needle, a big sponge, and some balls of wool. White, orange, lime green, and brown, I think."

Everything a needle felter would need to work on a project.

I flashback to when I walked Dina to the back door and picked green fibre off of her sweater.

The knot in my stomach grows bigger as I apply a bandage to my dad's injured finger. Something isn't right; something way bigger than Dina lying to me about her crafting habit. I feel like I'm missing something right in front of me.

"You were very brave," I tease. "Would you like a sticker, lollipop, or small toy?" I produce a basket from under the counter. We give them to the children of customers to keep them occupied while their parents shop.

"I'd like sushi and a glass of wine with my daughter," he says, chuckling. "But I'll take a grape lollipop to sustain me until we get there." He reaches into the basket and takes a purple lollipop.

Putting away the first aid kit, my phone dings.

April: I wasn't snooping, but when Dina went to the washroom, I *might* have nudged her table and woken up her laptop, then looked at the screen. Accidentally, of course.

Me: It sounds very unintentional.

April: I knew you'd understand.

Me: What did you see?

April: The unreleased Familia book.

Me: Are you sure?

April: I've read every book in the series. This is new. Wanna know which one of Mama's kids dies in the next book?

Me: NO SPOILERS!

April: It's weird that Dina has the unfinished book open on her laptop, right?

Me: It seems weird, but I don't know.

April: I keep wiping nearby tables so I can spy on her. Dina is definitely typing words into the book.

Me: I'm going out for lunch with my dad, then I'm coming to the bakery.

April: OK. I'll keep wiping and snooping. Artsy Tartsy will have the cleanest tables in town!

"Ready, Dad?" I ask, walking toward him.

His bandaged finger reminds me of the bandages on Dina's fingers. She said one of them was a paper cut, and the other was her nail-biting habit, but now I wonder if they were needle-felting injuries.

"Ready, Bean!" he replies, standing up.

"Dad, can I ask you a work question?" I ask, retrieving my purse from under the counter.

"Of course," he replies.

"Does your assistant ever work on your unfinished manuscripts?"

He shakes his head. "No," he replies with conviction. "No one reads my first draft except me. Zoe is my wife and one of my editors, and I don't even share my first drafts with her. My assistant never has writing-related tasks." He points to his chest. "I'm the author. I'm the only one who does writing-related tasks."

Claire claimed to be an avid needle felter, but showed no interest in the felting display at the store or in the felting supplies we sell. Dina claims she is not a needle felter, but showed enthusiastic interest in all things needle felting when she was here, and carries felting supplies in her backpack.

My dad says Claire wasn't an avid reader and preferred magazines to books. Dina is a self-described bookworm who totes 20 paperbacks in her backpack without breaking a sweat.

Dina is more Claire-like than Claire.

My dad and I say goodbye to Sophie and are about to leave the store when my phone rings.

"It's Eric," I tell my dad. "Just one more minute." I accept the call and put him on speaker.

"Hey, babe! How's your day?"

"Good. I'm just about to have lunch with my dad. He's right here. You're on speaker."

"Hello, Eric," my father shouts from right beside me.

"Hi, Mitchell," Eric responds. "I thought I'd call and give you the good news."

"You found Brooks?" I ask.

"Not yet." he replies. "Other good news. Forensics found peanut oil on some items we took from the cottage yesterday. I have a theory."

"We're dying to hear it," I say.

"Yes, Eric, you can't leave us with a cliffhanger," Mitchell shouts.

"We found peanut oil on the pages of several magazines," Eric divulges.

I remember picking up magazines at the cottage when Dina sent me to the doc to collect her things. Could he be talking about the same magazines?

"Were the magazines inside the den with Claire?" I ask.

"No," Eric replies. "They were in the washroom. I suspect Claire went from the office to the washroom where she came into contact with the magazines, then returned to the office. Her allergic reaction started after she locked the door."

"Are you saying Claire's death wasn't murder after all? It was an accident?" Dad yells.

"That's what I'm saying. And the coroner concurs. He's going to change Claire's death from murder to accidental."

"Eric, were the magazines on the edge of the bathtub?" I ask.

"They were."

"Are there fingerprints on the magazines?" I ask.

"From three people," he says with hesitation. "Why are you asking? You have that tone in your voice, like you've figured something out."

"Were the fingerprints Claire's, Brooks's, and mine?" I ask.

"That's right," Eric says. "But you aren't a suspect, babe. You were at the scene when you helped Dina pack. We expected to find your fingerprints there."

"I'm not worried about that." I shake my head even though Eric can't see me. "The only way Claire touched those magazines is if she went down to the dock." I explain to Eric how Brooks and I went to the dock on

Friday to fetch Dina's stuff when we were helping her pack. "I assumed the magazines were part of her stuff and brought them back to the cottage. Dina told us the magazines were already at the cottage when she and Claire arrived. Brooks put them on the edge of the tub. Dina seemed to avoid touching them. I remember our conversation clear as day. Dina mentioned she took the magazines down to the dock on Thursday. I commented it was a good thing it didn't rain since they were down there overnight."

"Why aren't Dina's fingerprints on the magazines?" Eric sighs on the other end of the phone. "If she took them to the dock, her fingerprints should be there."

"Because she doesn't want them to be?" I suggest.

"I have to locate Dina Langley."

I gasp. "I know where she is."

Panic radiates from the knot in my stomach to the rest of my body when I realize Dina is at Artsy Tartsy. With April. Alone. My best friend is alone with a murderer. My best friend is in danger.

"Stay here with Sophie," I instruct my dad as soon as Eric and I end our call.

"You aren't going there?" my dad asks, incredulous.

"And text April," I add, ignoring his question. "Tell her to unlock the back door without Dina noticing." I'd do it myself, but I'm not coordinated enough to run and text at the same time.

"This isn't a good idea, Bean. She's dangerous!"

"I'll be back soon." I shove my phone in my back

pocket, throw open the door, and run toward Artsy Tartsy.

I'm coming, April. If Dina plans to put up a fight, she'll have to go through both of us.

"Bean! Megan!" My dad's voice grows fainter the farther I run.

CHAPTER 24

I slow down to a walk a few doors from the bakery and catch my breath. I don't want to rush in there all flustered and tip off Dina.

"Hey, Megastar!" April flashes me a wide smile when I enter the bakery.

"Hey!" I say, smiling.

Her phone buzzes, and she looks down. The cheerful expression disappears from her face. Her brows furrow toward each other, and she swallows hard. She must have read the text my dad sent. April looks up at me with a blank expression on her face. I give her an exaggerated smile, reminding her to act natural. Picking up on my hint, April smiles, then snaps her fingers.

"I saved you a slice of pistachio cake with strawberry meringue," she says. "I'll just nip to the kitchen and get it."

"Sounds yummy," I say. "You and T spoil me." April disappears into the kitchen.

I'm sure the cake is an excuse to unlock the back door.

I cough to cover the clicking sound when I lock the front door. Then, keeping my eye on Dina the entire time to make sure she doesn't look up from her laptop screen, I flip the sign from OPEN to CLOSED.

Dina is laser-focused on her laptop. She hasn't looked up once since I walked in the door.

"Here you go, Megadoodle." April slides the plate and a glass of water across the counter to me.

"Thanks," I say, taking them, and sitting at the table behind Dina. "I can watch the bakery if you have paper-work to do in the office," I suggest. "I'm finished at Knitorious for the day."

Will April take the hint and leave through the back door she just unlocked? There's no point in both of us locking ourselves in here with a potential killer.

"Don't be silly," April responds. "I wouldn't ask you to do that." She shrugs. "Besides, the paperwork is all caught up."

She won't leave. I don't blame her. I wouldn't leave her alone, either. I give her a trace of a smile, and she winks in return.

"Hi, Dina," I exclaim.

Dina raises her index finger. "Just give me one minute." Her index finger returns to her laptop keyboard. I have a few mouthfuls of cake while April repeatedly wipes the same area of countertop. "And… done!" Dina slams her laptop shut, looks up at April with a satisfied grin, and says, "One lemon meringue tart, please!"

"Coming right up!" April says.

Dina spins around in her chair. "Hi, Megan!" She smiles at me. "April told me what happened at Knitorious last night. I couldn't believe it! Piper Peters broke in and tried to steal the *Familia* books?! It's a good thing we let your stepmum convince us to move them, huh?"

April places a plate in front of Dina, who says thank you and takes a big bite of tart.

"Yes," I agree. "And it's a good thing my neighbour noticed someone in the store."

"I can't believe Brooks told her where to find the books." Dina shakes her head. "With all the activity and confusion this weekend, I forgot to tell him we moved them. Thank goodness. Otherwise she might have tried to break into your house."

"Have you heard from Brooks?" I ask.

Dina shakes her head. "No. Not since we had lunch on Saturday. But I told the police I'll tell them if Brooks tries to contact me."

"Do you know if the police have found him yet?" she asks me.

"As far as I know, they're still looking," I reply. "But they almost caught up with him this morning. He was at Knitorious when I arrived."

"Inside?" Dina asks wide-eyed before putting the rest of the tart in her mouth.

I nod. "Inside. Brooks is a decent lock picker."

"Wow," she garbles with her mouth full of tart. "Maybe he picked the lock in the den at the rental cottage," she mumbles, her words difficult to understand. Then she swallows. "Did he try to hurt you? Are you OK?"

"I'm fine," I assure her. "He didn't harm me. He didn't even threaten to harm me. He wanted to talk."

"About what?" Dina asks.

"He wanted to clear his name. Brooks insists he did not kill Claire."

She rolls her eyes. "Of course, he does. He'll say anything to avoid jail."

"Dina," I say, about to change the subject. "My dad mentioned you had a felting needle and some fibre in your backpack yesterday. Why do you have them if you're not a felter?"

Dina looks down, avoiding eye contact with me. "They're Claire's," she confesses. "I took them from the rental cottage when we were there on Friday." She shrugs. "I wanted something of hers. Something important to her, but not expensive, you know?"

She's lying. The police checked our bags before and after we left the cottage. Dina did not have any needle felting supplies.

"Silly me. I thought the needle felting stuff belonged

to you," I laugh. "And your bandaged fingers resulted from needle-felting accidents." I laugh, and April laughs with me.

"Why would someone lie about a hobby like needle felting?" April asks with a shrug.

"Exactly," Dina agrees. "That wouldn't make any sense."

"You're right," I concur. "But something else doesn't add up," I suggest.

"What?" Dina asks, the smile disappearing from her face.

"According to Brooks, you suggested he approach Claire's family and offer to purchase the *Familia* rights from them. He says you even suggested it might help if Jules approached them because Claire's family are Jules Janssen fans."

"What?" she asks, overdramatizing her skepticism. "That's not true." Dina shakes her head. "Either he lied, or he misunderstood me," she insists. "Yes, I told him that Claire's family are huge Jules Janssen fans because it's true. But I didn't tell them to ask her family to sell the rights. I suggested it might mean a lot to them if Jules reached out personally and offered condolences for Claire's death. That's all I said, I swear." She's talking fast now. Too fast. She's rattled. "Remember, I told you I think it's tacky to talk to Claire's family about business while they're grieving. He's just angry because I refused to be part of their scheme."

"You're right," I reply. "Your version makes more sense." Relief washes across Dina's face. "Especially since Claire's family won't inherit the rights to *Familia*, you will."

"Me?" Dina pokes herself in the chest. "How do you know that?" She narrows her eyes and looks at me sideways.

I shrug. "I heard it somewhere. The rumour mill around here is incredibly accurate and efficient." I take a sip of water. "You don't seem shocked, Dina. Did you know Claire was bequeathing you the rights to her books?"

"To be honest, I'm not as shocked as I should be," Dina admits. "Claire must've left the rights to me because she knew I would respect her wishes and not sell them."

"Did the contract between you and Claire stipulate you would inherit the rights if she died?"

"Who told you about our contract?" She sounds defensive now.

"Brooks," I reply. "He mentioned it at the cottage. He didn't have many details, only knew a contract existed and said it made for a strange working relationship between you and Claire."

"We've already established that Brooks is a liar," Dina reminds me.

"Was he lying when he said the contract stipulates that when the Familia series ends, the working relationship between you and Claire also ends?" I ask. "When Claire announced the next *Familia* book would be the last, she essentially fired you over social media. It would be understandable if that made you angry."

"You don't understand what you're talking about," Dina says snidely. "Claire couldn't fire me, even if she wanted to." She glares at me through squinty eyes. "And the rights were never Claire's to bequeath."

"What does that mean?" I ask.

"Never mind." She dismisses my question with a flick of her wrist. "I don't want to talk about this anymore. You're making me feel like a suspect."

If the shoe fits...

"I'm sorry," I say. "I didn't mean to upset you. If it makes you feel better, I have it on very good authority that, as of fifteen minutes ago, there were no suspects in Claire Rivera's death."

This piques Dina's interest, and she inches her chair closer to my table.

"Did your boyfriend tell you that?" she asks. "Chief Sloane? What did he say?"

"If I tell you, it can't leave this bakery," I say.

Dina nods with enthusiasm. "Of course not." She makes an X over her chest with her index finger. "Cross my heart and hope to die."

"He said they found traces of peanut oil on some magazines at the cottage. Eric theorizes that Claire left the office, touched the magazines, then returned to the office, and died after she locked the door."

"So, he thinks Claire's death was accidental," she summarizes, smiling. Dina inhales a deep breath, then blows it out. "That's fantastic news! There's no murderer."

"That was as of fifteen minutes ago," I remind her. "As of ten minutes ago, we think there is a murderer."

"Who?"

"What did you and Claire argue about before she died?" I ask, ignoring her question.

"Claire didn't give me any warning before she sent out the social media post saying *Familia* was over," Dina reveals. "It took me by surprise, and I was angry." She sighs. "Just because we argued doesn't mean I killed her."

"Did Claire lock herself in the den to escape the argument?" I ask.

"No," Dina replies, looking me in the eye.

"So, you didn't expose Claire to peanut oil then lock her in the den, forcing her to use a felting needle to pick the lock and save herself?"

Dina sits back and crosses her arms in front of her chest. "How could I, when the only key was inside the den with her?"

"You're the only witness who claims there was only one key," I challenge. "No one else can remember. The cleaner didn't notice how many keys were there. The landlord didn't notice how many keys were there when he inspected the cottage between renters. The previous tenants aren't sure whether there was one key or two because they claim they didn't lock the den during their stay."

"There you go." Dina shrugs. "You can't prove there was a second key."

"You're right," I accede. "But people don't notice things unless they change. If there are always two keys and one key is missing, it would stand out, and the cleaner or the landlord would notice. If both keys were there, neither would notice because nothing was out of place."

Dina shakes her head and laughs. "I don't think your theory will be admissible in court." She lurches forward and puts her forearms on my table, causing me to flinch. From the corner of my eye, April startles behind the counter. "What motive would I have to kill Claire? Why destroy a job I love sooner than I have to?"

"Maybe you were so angry that you weren't thinking straight," I suggest, hoping to give her an opening to confess. "Or maybe this super-secret contract you and Claire had would be void if she died." I slide my chair back a little in case my next statement tips Dina over the edge. "Or maybe with the rights to *Familia*, you wouldn't have to worry about finding another job."

"I already told you the rights weren't Claire's," she snarls. "Claire and I were friends. We'd worked together since before the first book came out. I wouldn't kill my friend."

"Claire told me you weren't friends," I counter. "If I recall, her exact words were, *we're barely friends*."

"I would *never* put *Familia* at risk." Dina bangs the table with her fist, her face flushed with angry heat. "I love the Familia series just as much as Claire did."

"I think you're lying," I accuse.

"What?" she says through clenched teeth.

"I think you love the Familia series *more* than Claire did." Confusion clouds Dina's face. "Because you're the author and Claire was your assistant."

"You sound ridiculous," she hisses, rolling her eyes and shaking her head. "Utter nonsense."

"Let's look at the facts," I suggest, counting on my fingers. "The author of *Familia* is a needle felter. There is zero evidence Claire was a needle felter, whereas you have needle felting supplies in your backpack." I lower one finger. "Claire studied graphic design, and you have a Master of Fine Arts degree in creative writing." I lower another finger. "Claire never talked about her dream of being a writer until after she released the first *Familia* book. You are a lifelong booklover who studied writing." I lower my third finger. "Claire wasn't much of a reader except for gossip magazines. You are a bookworm and always have multiple books and ebooks with you." I lower my fourth finger.

Dina holds up her hands in surrender. "OK, Nancy Drew, you win." She laughs. "I'll admit it. I'm the ghost writer behind the *Familia* books. All of them."

A ghost writer is someone who is paid to write for

the named author. Ghost writing is surprisingly common. It's almost always a secret because ghost writers aren't credited for their work, and they sign contracts swearing them to secrecy about what they write and for whom. Fun fact: all the Nancy Drew books were ghost written by different, uncredited authors. The credited author, Carolyn Keene, is a pen name for the many authors who contributed to the series.

"Why?" I ask. "Why didn't you take credit for your own work? You're such a talented writer."

After a deep sigh and contemplative look that makes me think she's not sure how much to tell me, Dina runs her hands through her blonde hair and speaks.

"I was very young when I thought up the idea for the Familia series," she explains. "I wrote the first three books when I was still a teenager. Literary agents wouldn't take me seriously. Most of them didn't believe I was the author because of my age. When I approached Brooks, I lied and told him I worked for the author, so he wouldn't write me off because of my age like everyone else. He liked my books, and I didn't want to ruin it by meeting him in person and having him realize how young I was. So, I hired a lawyer who helped me find and hire Claire. She had the skills to act as my author assistant, and she had the perfect personality to represent the books. We hired her away from your father." Dina touches my hand, and I suppress a wince and fight the urge to yank it away. "I always felt guilty about that. Especially after your father accused us of stealing his idea."

"Did you steal his idea?" I ask.

"No," Dina insists, "and I can prove it. By the time I hired Claire, I had already written the first three books in the series. My series predates your father's idea." She shrugs. "It was an unfortunate coincidence." I slide my hand out from under hers. "Anyway," she says. "The lawyer was the only person who knew about our arrangement. Everything happened so fast after Claire was onboard. Brooks met her and took her on as a client. We got a publishing deal. Then the first book was released, and it was an enormous success. We were stuck. The world believed Claire was the author, and I was her assistant. It terrified us that if we told the truth, the fans might not trust us anymore, and it would ruin *Familia*."

"Claire must have wanted to end your arrangement badly if she announced the end of the Familia series without checking with you first."

"She wanted out for the past couple of years," Dina admits, "but I kept convincing her to stay. Claire started to believe our lie. She wanted to write her own books and publish them under her own name. The woman had written nothing longer than an email, but she knew that because she was Claire Rivera, best-selling author in over twenty countries, whatever she wrote would earn money. She would have published poorly written books and earned money because of the success she had with my writing. She was planning to profit from my hard work. I couldn't let that happen." Dina stops talking, like she realizes she might say something she couldn't take back.

"How did you stop her?" April asks, leaning on the counter, engrossed in Dina's version of events.

She crosses her arms in front of her chest. "You can't prove I killed Claire! Anyway, how could I have killed Claire? I was sitting on the dock when she died. There were eyewitnesses, the neighbours saw me. And I was on the phone with my parents."

"I think you went down to the dock after Claire's anaphylaxis started, or maybe even after she died," I hypothesize. "I think you already laced the magazine pages with peanut oil and left them in the den where Claire would find them. You knew Claire would read them because she loved gossip magazines. When Claire ran into the den and locked the door to escape your argument, she flipped through the pages of at least one magazine and ingested the peanut oil when she licked her fingers to turn the pages. I think you held the door closed from the outside so Claire couldn't escape and save herself. She probably thought the key wasn't working and tried to pick the lock with the felting needle *you* left in the den."

"Oooooh, you're so close," Dina says, her words laced with a bizarre sense of smug satisfaction. "I sensed Claire was planning to do something drastic to end our arrangement. I bought a bunch of mind-numbing gossip magazines and laced them with peanut oil, just like you said. I scattered them around the cottage when we arrived. I wore gloves when I touched them so they could never be traced back to me. Claire didn't go near the magazines. She kept playing games on her stupid phone and texting her lame friends."

Dina rolls her eyes. "She'd do anything to avoid reading. Anyway, when she posted the social media message that destroyed my career, we had a huge argument. It was nasty, and we both said horrible things. Claire ran into the den to escape and locked the door. After we had time to calm down, I knocked on the door. She didn't answer. I used the second key to let myself in. Claire was in the throes of anaphylaxis. She couldn't speak. She was writhing on the floor, looking at me with desperate, pleading eyes. I told her I would get her EpiPen. I promised I would be right back. I put on latex gloves, took her phone and both keys, and left. I locked the door behind me. I walked around the cottage and gathered up the magazines I'd laced with peanut oil. Then I got the peanut oil from my room. I put my ear up to the den door, and it was silent. I knocked and called her name. Nothing. I unlocked the door.

"I promised myself if Claire was still alive, I would save her. She wasn't. I had to squeeze past the door because she died right behind it. I left her phone and one key on the desk, then removed the peanut-oil-laced magazine she touched. I locked the door behind me with the second key. At the dock, I took off the rubber gloves, placed the key and the small jar of peanut oil inside them, and tied them shut. I skipped rocks while I figured out what to do next. The neighbours came out. We said hi. They went back to their cottage, and while I was throwing rocks, I threw the glove into the lake, then phoned my parents. I wasn't sure how to dispose of the magazines. I decided not to. My fingerprints aren't on them. I made sure I never touched them. The police will never link them to me."

"Yes, we will," Eric says from the doorway between the bakery and kitchen.

He tells Dina that she's under arrest and reads out her rights. Two other officers cuff and search her.

The police escort Dina to a waiting patrol car, and April and I fall into each other's arms. We scold each other for taking risks; her for refusing to leave when I gave her the chance, and me for goading a disturbed killer instead of waiting for the police to arrive.

"Bean! Never scare me like that again!" My dad chastises as he puts his arms around April and me. "I can only handle this much excitement in a book, not my daughter's life!"

"Why are you here? You were supposed to stay with Sophie," I say.

"Would you stay with the corgi if Hannah ran down the street chasing a murderer?" he asks.

He makes a good point.

Eric asks April and me if we're OK, then tells us we need to give statements.

"Well done, Eric!" My dad hugs him, which takes Eric, and the rest of us, by surprise. "Good job, son!"

April, Eric, and I exchange a look in silent agreement never to tell Adam about Mitchell calling Eric, *son*.

"Thank you, sir, but I can't take all the credit. I have a brilliant partner." He winks at me.

CHAPTER 25

MONDAY, April 26th

I trap a crab sashimi with my chopsticks and dip it into the soya sauce before popping it into my mouth.

"I'm glad we finally got to have our sushi lunch," my dad says between salmon-avocado rolls.

"I'm glad you extended your trip for a few days so we could make it happen," I reply.

"I was on a roll," he says, laughing. He holds up a salmon-avocado roll between his chopsticks. "Pardon the pun." I groan at his attempt to be punny. "I didn't want to interrupt my flow by packing up and driving away," he says. "Can you believe I finished the first draft of the next book and submitted it early for a change? They're probably still in shock at my publisher's office." We laugh.

"Whatever the reason, it was nice to have you and Zoe around for a few extra days," I say.

"We might be back sooner than you think. Eric said if Dina goes to trial, I might have to testify." He sounds excited at the prospect.

"It was just a warning," I tell him. "I've been a witness in more than one murder case since Eric and I met, and I haven't stepped inside a courtroom yet." I shrug one shoulder. My dad lets out a disappointed sigh. "He thinks Dina will take a deal," I say. "The evidence against her is solid."

After Dina confessed, the police searched the lake at the rental cottage and found the latex gloves with the key to the den and the bottle of peanut oil inside. Both the key and the bottle had Dina's fingerprints on them.

When he searched her credit card transactions, Eric discovered where and when Dina purchased the magazines. The store where she bought them provided surveillance video of her purchase to the police.

The cleaner and landlord at the rental cottage confirmed there were no magazines at the cottage prior to Claire's and Dina's arrival. The landlord has a strict rule about removing personal items and food left by previous renters before the new renters arrive. The cleaner confirmed she strictly enforces this rule and removed any trace of the previous renters.

When the cyber crimes unit searched Dina's computer, they found manuscripts for three unpublished *Familia* books. Dina admitted she planned to claim she found the manuscripts after Claire's death. She hoped to convince the publisher to publish them posthumously, extending the life of the Familia book series. Sadly, it's unlikely they'll ever get published now.

The lawyer who helped Dina find and hire Claire to be the credited author of the Familia series provided a copy of their contract to the police. Dina was telling the truth; she was the author, and Claire was her assistant, whose duties included being the credited author of the books and the public face of the series. Claire was well paid for her part in the scheme, and she and Dina shared the rights to the Familia series, with a clause that, in the event of Claire's death, Claire's half of the film rights would revert to Dina. Selling the film rights would have been a complication that neither woman wanted. It would have risked exposing their arrangement.

"If there is a trial, will the British woman fly back to testify?" my dad asks.

"You mean Piper Peters?" I confirm.

He nods. "Yes, the lady with the mourning attire. Such an intriguing persona." He winks. "She might inspire a character in a future book."

"I don't know," I admit. "I'll have to ask Eric. Maybe she could testify over video chat or something."

Piper avoided charges in relation to the break-and-enter at Knitorious in exchange for her immediate departure to England and a signed oath that she won't come back. If she does, she'll face charges for the crimes she committed. Eric was so eager for her to leave that he confirmed with the airline she had boarded her flight.

"What about Claire's agent?" my dad asks, dipping a California roll into some soya sauce. "I hope he faces the consequences of breaking into your store."

"He won't," I tell my dad. "I don't want him to. He didn't hurt anyone or damage anything. I just want to put this entire book fair behind us and move on."

Piper's partner-in-crime, Brooks Wiley, turned himself into police as soon as he heard about Dina's arrest.

True to her word, Jules Janssen and her entourage cooperated with the investigation and provided statements that eliminated Brooks as having any involvement in Claire's death. He wasn't charged with breaking into Knitorious because I asked Eric to let it go; Brooks wasn't a threat to me, and the last thing I want to do is give another statement. He also avoided charges for his role in conspiring with Piper to steal the books because that would require Piper's testimony, and Eric isn't keen to engage her ever again. Last I heard, Brooks was working and travelling with Jules; he's become part of her entourage.

"Are Brooks and the movie star still an item?" my dad asks.

"I have no idea," I admit. "But Adam said she called him to discuss making a movie in Harmony Lake."

I tell my dad how Jules Janssen gave up her pursuit of the *Familia* film rights and, instead, is working on a film inspired by Claire's murder. She contacted Adam to talk to him about filming part of it in Harmony Lake. The film is a fictionalized version of events. They'll change names and places to avoid lawsuits and such. Adam says Jules plans to play the role of Dina. I wonder who will play me?

"I wonder who will play me?" my dad asks; great minds think alike.

"Why would you be in it?" I ask.

He shrugs. "Why wouldn't I?" he answers my question with a question.

I check the time on my phone. "We better get a wiggle on, Dad. Zoe is waiting for you, and if you don't hit the road soon, you'll find yourself driving at night."

"I don't enjoy driving at night," he says, shoving the last piece of sushi in his mouth.

WE WALK BACK to Knitorious because that's where I parked the car, but when we get there, everyone is waiting outside in the parking lot.

"I thought we were leaving from chez Martel?" my dad asks Zoe.

"We were, but I grew tired of waiting for you," she says. "The car is packed, and we have to get on the road. We don't want to stop for the night at a hotel."

"I'm not doing that again." He chuckles. "Last time we ended up in the middle of a murder investigation."

Dad and Zoe take turns saying goodbye to everyone, starting with Sophie, who is excited that her favourite people are all here. Next, they hug and kiss Connie and Archie, then April and Tamara, who give them a box of baked goodies for the road. Next, they move on to Adam. Zoe gives Adam a warm hug and kisses him on the cheek. My dad shakes Adam's hand and pats his shoulder—which is practically a hug—and thanks him again for his help. Zoe gives me a tight squeeze and promises they'll come back before fall. I tell her I'll hold her to it. I thank her for all the cooking and mothering she always squeezes into our visits. She moves onto Eric and gives him a hug and cheek kiss. When my dad hugs me goodbye, he slips a small USB drive into my hand.

"What's this?" I ask, holding up the drive.

"It's the first draft of my next book," he replies.

"But no one gets to read your first draft," I remind him of his own words. "Never."

"I'm making an exception," he says. "You and Eric may read it." He winks. "I can't wait to hear what you think of it."

We wave them off, and after Mitchell and Zoe drive away, we scatter, exhausted from the week's events. Adam goes back to the town hall, April and Tamara return to their bakery, and Connie and Archie go home. Eric and I head upstairs to his apartment.

"Piper was right about one thing," I say, sinking into the leather sofa. "Your peace lily is much happier in its new location." I nod toward the plant that has sprouted blooms since Piper moved it.

"Maybe it would have bloomed on the windowsill," he responds, sitting next to me. "We'll never know."

I hold up the USB drive between us. "Who gets to read it first?" I ask.

He takes the drive from me and looks at it up close. "Let's read it together," he suggests. "Then we'll discover at the same time how your father kills me in his new book." He gets up and retrieves his laptop from the breakfast bar.

"He might not kill you," I say in defence of my dad.

"I interrogated him and told him he was a suspect," Eric reminds me. "I think my literary death is a done deal."

"You also eliminated him as a suspect, caught the real culprit, and love his daughter."

"I planned to ask your dad for permission to propose to you," Eric admits. "But I decided against it."

"Against asking Mitchell's permission, or against proposing?" I tease, knowing it's the former, not the latter.

"Against asking Mitchell," he clarifies. "I know it's traditional to ask the bride's father, but nothing about our relationship or family is traditional. I was asking the wrong person."

"You were," I agree. I'm about to launch into a lecture and tell him I'm a forty-one-year-old woman who makes her own decisions, and he doesn't need anyone's permission to propose to me other than mine.

Before I open my mouth he says, "I need to ask Hannah and Connie."

Sigh. Eric is traditional at heart. He wants to do things right. He's eager for us to get married, but he's waiting for me to be ready, which I'm not. Yet. Soon, though.

"I hope our life goes back to boring now that the book fair is over, and you solved Claire's murder," I say, eager to change the subject.

"You mean, *we* solved Claire's murder," he corrects me and inserts the USB drive into his computer. "It'll be nice and boring until the next murder." He chuckles.

I swat his arm. "That's not funny," I say. "You'll tempt fate saying stuff like that."

"I'm sure fate would agree that we've solved our share of murders," he reassures me. "I have a feeling life will be wonderfully boring from now on."

I wish I had the same feeling.

EPILOGUE

Eric and I finished reading the first draft of my dad's book, *Shark Attack: Fresh Blood*.

Good news: He didn't kill Eric. Bad news: He killed Adam. Again.

The protagonist, Rock Granite, is ready to retire but not ready to give up on capturing Alan Mandell, AKA The Shark. Rock takes on two proteges, Aaron Stone and Michelle Moldavite. Aaron's physique and strength are imposing, and he has experience in personal combat, while Michelle is clever and saves them from dangerous situations by outwitting their opponents. The chemistry between Aaron and Michelle is intense, but they try to ignore it. They have a Springer Spaniel sidekick named Stella.

Aaron and Michelle take up the mantle of hunting The Shark while the retired Rock Granite acts as their mentor and guide. Just like Rock Granite, Aaron and

Michelle track down The Shark, and their final confrontation results in The Shark's apparent demise, though his body is not found.

Not only did Mitchell not kill Eric, but he made Eric a hero.

KEEP READING for a sneak peek of Rest In Fleece: A Knitorious Murder Mystery book 8.

REST IN FLEECE

CHAPTER 1

Saturday, June 12th

Shanice Bickerson rules her domain with awe-inspiring efficiency and a blind, three-legged Jack Russell Terrier named Kilian. She has an important job. As head librarian at the Harmony Lake Public Library, Mrs. Bickerson is a pillar of our community and one strand of the fibre that weaves our tight-knit community together.

The Harmony Lake Public Library is a hub of our small town. When residents visit the library, they get more than books. Mrs. Bickerson fosters a haven of community, companionship, and offers programs for residents of all ages.

"I'll be right with you, Megan," Mrs. Bickerson says, smiling and holding up her index finger.

"No worries," I reply.

But she doesn't hear me. Mrs. Bickerson's attention

is focussed on her husband, Boris Bickerson. They're standing at the periodical shelves. Mr. Bickerson crosses his arms in front of his broad chest and furrows his brow. His bushy mustache twitches when he speaks. Mrs. Bickerson's hands are on her hips, and she's shaking her head at whatever Mr. Bickerson is saying. The Bickersons are bickering.

Leaning against the counter, I pretend to browse the display of community flyers while discreetly monitoring the Bickersons in my peripheral vision.

Mr. Bickerson uncrosses his arms and gesticulates animatedly. Mrs. Bickerson throws up her hands in frustration and walks away while he's mid-sentence. Mr. Bickerson stomps his foot, scoffs, and marches out of the building.

"Sorry about that, Megan," Mrs. Bickerson says with a warm smile. Despite their domestic drama, Mrs. Bickerson remains poised. "How can I help you?" She pats her short, black, curly hair, then corrects her posture and squares her shoulders.

"I have a couple of blankets for you," I respond, smiling and placing a bag on the counter. "I have three today and should have more next week."

Mrs. Bickerson peeks inside the bag. "Wonderful!" she exclaims. "Thank you so much for doing this. The more isolated residents in our community love getting these lap blankets."

"Don't thank me," I insist. "All I do is crochet the squares together. It's The Charity Knitting Guild members who knit the squares and organize every-thing. I'm just their delivery service."

The Charity Knitting Guild teamed up with the Harmony Lake Public Library for their current project: lap blankets for the Outreach Reading Program. Every week, Mrs. Bickerson gathers books and magazines from the library and visits residents who can't get to the library as often as they'd like. This month, she's giving them a lap blanket with their book of choice.

The charity knitters knit the squares and drop them off at my yarn store, Knitorious. I use some yarn and a crochet hook to crochet the squares together into lap blankets, then drop them off at the library.

"It's wonderful having Hannah here, by the way," Mrs. Bickerson informs me as she stashes the bag of blankets somewhere under the counter. "I'm so happy she's working at the library this summer."

"She's happy to be here," I respond. "Thank you for letting me borrow her until the end of the month." It feels and sounds odd to thank someone for lending me my daughter.

Hannah is almost twenty. She just finished her second year of university in Toronto and is home for the summer. She has a summer job at the library, but Mrs. Bickerson let me borrow her until the end of the month while my two part-time employees sip their way through the vineyards of Italy and France on a wine crawl.

Mrs. Bickerson giggles. "It's the least I can do." She

gestures somewhere below the counter. "These blankets mean more than you know to the people who receive them."

Mr. Bickerson stomps back into the library, glances at Mrs. Bickerson, then sneers at Kilian who is resting on a dog bed near the door. Mr. Bickerson huffs, turns, and stomps out again.

I lean over the counter and lower my voice. "Is Mr. Bickerson OK?"

Mrs. Bickerson rolls her eyes and flicks her wrist dismissively. "He's angry about the money I spent on Mysti," she explains. "But she's worth every penny. I get more value from the time I spend with Mysti than Boris gets from the time he spends fishing and listening to stock market podcasts."

"Mysti?" I ask.

"You know," she replies, "the fortune teller who set up a booth at the lakefront?"

"I've seen her around, but I haven't met her," I say.

The town is abuzz about the mysterious fortune teller who arrived here last week. Some people say she's blessed with a gift, and some say she's a con artist whose only gift is separating the residents of Harmony Lake from their money.

"Oh, Megan, you must pay her a visit!"

"Fortune telling isn't my thing..." I start.

"Mysti's gift goes way beyond telling fortunes," Mrs. Bickerson interrupts, her eyes wide with enthusiasm and her voice hopeful. She leans into me. "Mysti can contact the dead," she adds in a whisper.

"Really?" I ask, skeptical and concerned at the same time.

"My parents send messages through her," she whispers, then gives me an exaggerated nod.

Mrs. Bickerson's parents passed away last year, a few months apart, after living long, happy lives. The Bickersons were their caregivers, and the double loss was hard for Mrs. Bickerson. Their deaths left Mrs. Bickerson with an empty nest. The Bickerson children are adults and out in the world, living their lives. Following her parents' deaths, Mrs. Bickerson transferred her maternal fussing to the library. The town benefits, but I'm not sure Mrs. Bickerson does.

"I'm glad you find comfort in your visits to Mysti." I smile, sympathetic to her situation.

My mother died when I was twenty-one. She died shortly after Hannah was born, when I needed a mother more than ever. Almost twenty years later, I still have moments when I would give anything to see her, hear her voice, or ask her for advice.

I hope Mysti isn't exploiting Mrs. Bickerson's grief for money. But if Mrs. Bickerson finds comfort from the "messages" Mysti gives her, maybe it isn't a waste of money.

"Well," I say, pushing myself off the counter and pulling myself up to my full height, "I should get back.

Hannah is alone at the store. I hope you and Mr. Bickerson work things out."

"There's nothing to work out," Mrs. Bickerson says, resolute. "Mysti's gift is priceless. You cannot put a price on the peace of mind she provides."

On my way out, I stop to visit Kilian. When I put my hand in front of his nose, he wags his tail and looks in my direction with his closed eyes, sniffing the air. I tell him he's a good boy, give him a few head rubs and a scratch between the ears.

Today is one of the first summer-like days of the year. The sun is bright, the air is hot, and a warm breeze blows off the lake. I lower my sunglasses from my head to my face and stroll down Water Street toward Knitorious. The sidewalk is busy with smiling people soaking up the sun and window shopping. On the other side of the street, walkers, joggers, dogs, kids, and strollers dot the lakefront park.

I'm wearing my first sundress of the season. Sundresses are one of my many guilty pleasures. Despite living where it's winter up to six months of the year, I have an extensive sundress collection. Today's selection is an off-the-shoulder maxi dress with purple and blue flowers.

I'm a few stores away from Knitorious when its door opens.

"Megastar! There you are!" April calls, her impossibly long legs skipping toward me. "Hannah said you went to the library." She hooks her arm through mine.

April likes to come up with nicknames that sound like puns of my actual name.

"I did," I confirm. "And now I'm going back to work."

"Not yet." April grins, veering us off the sidewalk and onto the curb. She looks both ways then drags me, running, across Water street.

"Where are we going?" I ask.

"To find out the future," April replies. "There's a fortune teller reading tarot cards in the park. I thought it would be a laugh!"

I love April. She was my first friend in Harmony Lake. We've been best friends since our daughters were in diapers. We met at a mummy-and-me playgroup when I moved here. Our daughters are best friends too. They attend the same university.

"I have to get back to the store," I protest. "Hannah's been alone for a while..."

"The store is empty," April argues. "Hannah said it's been dead all day. She gave me her blessing to kidnap you for as long as I want."

April takes long strides, and I trot to keep up with her. April is tall, and I am short. We're kindred spirits, but physical opposites. She's blonde, I'm brunette. Her hair is straight, mine is curly. Her eyes are blue, mine are hazel. April has a perpetual tan, and I look anemic. I'm not anemic, I just look that way. April's tall, lean body looks like it just stepped off a runway at a Milan fashion show, while I'm shorter and curvy with round hips, big boobs, and a small waist.

"I'm not wearing any SPF," I declare, worried about my exposed shoulders.

"You'll be fine," April assures me. "She's reading tarot cards under a tree. We'll be in the shade."

"I don't believe in fortune tellers and psychics," I protest.

April shrugs. "It's for fun. It's just entertainment. We won't make major life decisions based on what she tells us."

"Do you believe in supernatural stuff?" I ask.

She shrugs again. "I don't know. I mean, I'm open minded. If that makes sense. On one hand, I like to think there's a plan, and all this"—she gestures around us—"isn't just random chaos. But I also like to think we control our own destinies."

This conversation is too deep for a Saturday morning.

The fortune teller is under a huge sugar maple tree. She has a large blanket laid out with a crystal ball, tarot cards, and crystals placed around the perimeter in a circle. A handwritten sign leans against the tree. MYSTI CALLY ~ SPIRITUAL HEALER ~ GUIDE ~ SOOTHSAYER

"Is that Mr. Bickerson?" April asks, lifting her sunglasses and squinting to confirm her sighting.

"Looks like it," I reply. "I saw him at the library earlier, and he was wearing the same outfit. And his moustache is twitching like when he was bickering with Mrs. Bickerson."

"I'd never guess he's into predicting the future and having his tarot cards read," April observes.

"He's not," I confirm.

I tell her about the heated exchange between Mr. and Mrs. Bickerson, and Mrs. Bickerson's confession that they argued about how much money Mrs. Bickerson spends on Mysti.

We keep a respectable distance and watch their interaction from the shade of a nearby oak tree. They seem oblivious to us, and their discussion appears to escalate into a disagreement. The longer they talk, the more exaggerated their facial expressions become, and their body language grows increasingly defensive. Both parties have their arms crossed in front of them and only uncross them to point or gesture at the other person.

Mr. Bickerson takes an aggressive step toward Mysti and enters her personal space. She seems intimidated and backs up. He steps forward again.

"Is everything OK here?" April shouts, taking long strides to bridge the gap between the shade of our oak tree and the shade of their sugar maple.

I hustle to catch up to her, like a toddler chasing their mother.

"I was just telling this charlatan that the residents of this town don't appreciate her and her con-artist trickery setting up shop here," Mr. Bickerson booms.

"I think she got the message," I say, smiling.

"I doubt it," Mr. Bickerson says, then looks at April and me. "I'd advise you ladies to keep an eye on your wallets." He takes a deep breath and lets it out. "Have a pleasant afternoon."

April and I say goodbye to Mr. Bickerson's back as he storms away.

"Are you OK?" April asks Mysti.

"I'm fine." Mysti's trembling hands say otherwise. "Some people don't like the messages they receive." She shrugs. "But I can't control what the spirits tell me. I'm just the messenger."

We sit on Mysti's blanket, inside the crystal circle, and decide April will go first. While Mysti shuffles her deck of tarot cards and recites some kind of incantation under her breath, I take in our surroundings. A woman on a nearby bench is reading a book. Her gorgeous sundress catches my attention. It's flowy and a beautiful vivid yellow. The wide brim of her straw sunhat hides her face. She's also wearing sunglasses. I can't distinguish her features. Her nails are the same shade of yellow as her dress. Admiring her dress, I realize the sundress isn't the only thing catching my interest. She's wearing a wide-brimmed sunhat and sunglasses *in the shade*. And she hasn't turned the page of her book the entire time I've been watching. It's odd. It's almost like she's trying to go unnoticed, but she's trying so hard, it's backfiring and making her stand out.

"Earth to Megatron," April says, bringing me back

to the here and now. "It's your turn. Mysti wants you to shuffle the deck."

"Right," I say, picking up the oversized cards. "Sorry, my mind wandered."

The cards are too large for my hands, but I attempt to shuffle them before handing them back to Mysti.

"It's not really about the shuffling," Mysti explains, taking the cards and giving them a proper shuffle. "It's more about you having contact with the cards so they can absorb your energy." She smiles.

Mysti is pretty. She has long, light brown, wavy hair and small freckles spray the bridge of her nose. Her brown eyes and smile are warm. Unlike Mr. Bickerson, I don't pick up a dishonest or predatory vibe. She seems timid and vulnerable to me. The word *lonely* comes to mind. I'd guess she's in her late twenties, but her high-pitched, child-like voice makes her sound younger and adds to her air of vulnerability.

Mysti lays out three cards: The Page of Cups, The Tower, and Death.

At first glance, my future doesn't look very optimistic.

"The page is a young man," Mysti interprets, pointing to the first card. "Pages are messengers. This young man will bring you a message."

"A good message or a bad message?" April asks, fully immersed in the experience.

Mysti points to the tower card next to the page of cups and makes eye contact with me. "A message that will turn your world upside down and shake you to your foundation."

"Sounds ominous," I respond.

"Not necessarily," Mysti says. "Sometimes good news rocks our world too. And sometimes something that seems negative at first turns out to be a blessing in disguise."

So much wisdom from one so young.

"What about the death card?" I ask, nodding toward it.

"The death card rarely signifies a literal death," she explains with a chortle. "The death card usually portends a transition from one state to another. Something ends so something new can begin."

"But it can signify an actual death, right?" April clarifies.

"It can," Mysti replies, then looks at me. "But you have to consider the cards around it. A young man will give you a message that will turn your world upside down, and things will never be the same. I can't say if the change will be good or bad."

"When can I expect this young man to bring me this message?" I ask.

Mysti shrugs. "Sooner than you think."

Chapter 2

"It was vague. It could mean anything," I say to April in response to her enthusiasm about a mysterious young man showing up any second with a life-changing message. "This is how they operate. My fortune could apply to anyone. About anything. It's a setup, so the next time I talk to any young man, and he tells me anything, I'll believe Mysti's prediction came true and rush back to her with more money."

"She seemed sincere, Megnolia," April insists, opening the door to Knitorious and gesturing for me to go ahead of her. "I'm not saying it's true, I'm suggesting we keep our minds open to the possibility."

"Hey, Hannah Banana," I say to my daughter who's standing behind the counter. I scan the floor around my feet, expecting to find a dog clamouring for my attention. "Where's Sophie?"

Sophie is my corgi. She comes to work with me.

"Eric picked her up. They went to the dog park," Hannah replies. "He said to tell you they won't be long."

Eric Sloane is my boyfriend, dog walker, and the chief of our local police department.

"Was it busy?" I ask, stashing my purse under the counter.

"Other than Aunt April and Eric, only one person came in."

"Do you want to take your lunch?" I ask.

Hannah shakes her head and raises her eyebrows like she knows a secret.

When she shakes her head, her long curls bounce and sway around her shoulders. Hannah has my hair, except her curls are tighter. She also has my eye shape, but her green eyes are a blend of my hazel eyes and her dad's blue eyes. Lucky for her, Hannah inherited some height from her dad, so she's a couple of inches taller than me. We have the same fair skin, and similar hourglass figures. She can thank both of us for her sarcastic sense of humour. I like to take credit for her resourcefulness and intelligence.

"Someone is waiting to see Eric," Hannah says. "He got here a few minutes ago."

April pokes my rib. "A mysterious man," she whispers. "The Page of Cups."

I give the empty store a cursory glance. "Where is he?"

"He's in the back." Hannah jerks her head toward the backroom. "I thought the fewer people who see him the better."

"Why?" I ask.

"You'll see," she replies.

"Did you text Eric?" I ask.

"Not yet. I wanted to wait for you."

April sighs. "I should get back to the bakery."

April and her wife, Tamara, own Artsy Tartsy, the local bakery. Tamara is a talented pastry chef, and her creations are locally famous. They spoil me with treats.

"I should talk to the mystery man." April and I hug. "Thanks for the glimpse into our futures."

"Aunt April," Hannah blurts out. "You should go with Mum."

Now I'm equal parts concerned and curious. What the heck is going on?

"Do you have time?" I ask April.

"I do now," April replies, her curiosity piqued.

"Maybe Mysti's prediction is coming true," April whispers when we're almost at the door that separates the store from the backroom and kitchenette.

"Doubtful," I whisper in response.

A young man wearing a baseball cap sits at the table in the kitchenette. His head is lowered, and he's focussed on his cell phone. Because of his brimmed cap, I can't make out his face.

"Hi there," I say.

The young man's head jolts up from his phone. Our eyes meet. I hitch my breath to stop a gasp from escaping me and reach out, clutching April's forearm to steady myself. Blinking, I do a double take, stunned by the young man sitting in front of me.

"Holy smokes," April mutters under her breath, "they're identical."

I acknowledge her remark with a barely discernible nod.

"Hi. I'm Jaxon Squires." The young man stands up and takes off his green baseball cap. "You can call me Jax."

Even their voices sound hauntingly similar.

Speechless, I reach out by instinct and shake his

extended hand. When he smiles, my knees feel like they might give out. Jaxon Squires is the spitting image of Eric. The resemblance is undeniable. He has Eric's brown hair and eyes, complete with honey-coloured flecks, and Eric's smile. This is what Eric would have looked like twenty years ago. They're even the same height and have the same muscular build. *What's going on? Who is this boy?*

"Megan," I mumble, pulling my hand back. April touches my back reassuringly. I clear my throat. "I'm Megan Martel." I introduce myself in a clearer voice, and plaster a smile on my face. "What can I do for you, Jax?"

"The lady at the library said I might find Eric Sloane here," Jax replies with a nervous chuckle. He rubs the back of his neck the same way Eric does when he's nervous or embarrassed. "I went to the police station, but they said he's not working today. I didn't want to leave a message, so I tried the library." He shrugs. "I thought they might have a town directory or something with Eric's address. The librarian said I should try here."

I pull out a chair and sit at the small table, gesturing for Jax to join me. April joins us, too, sitting in the chair beside me. At a loss for words, I can't stop staring at this Eric-identical young man.

"Is Eric expecting you?" April asks, taking the conversational reins while I compose myself and recover from the shock.

"I doubt it," Jax replies. "We've never met." He wipes his palms on his denim-covered thighs and does his nervous chuckle again. "In fact, I'm pretty sure he doesn't know I exist."

"Why are you looking for him?" I ask, afraid I already know the answer.

"Eric Sloane is my father."

I inhale deeply and hold it. Jax's phone dings, and he looks at it. His facial muscles tense as he reads the screen.

"Is everything OK, Jax?" April asks.

Thank goodness she's here to be my voice when I can't speak.

"Yeah. Kind of," he replies. "A friend of mine is having an issue." He scans the room and nods toward the back door. "Can I use that door? I just want to call my friend to make sure everything's OK." He stands up.

"Of course," I say. "I'll text Eric while you're gone."

"So, I came to the right place?" Jax's eyes brighten with enthusiasm. "Awesome. Thank you. I'll be right back." He smiles.

"Eric has a son?" April hisses when the back door shuts with a thud.

"He's never mentioned it," I respond. "April, if Eric has a son, I don't think he knows."

"The resemblance is incredible. They could be…"

"Father and son?" I ask, finishing her sentence.

"I was going to say twins," she says. "But there's your page of cups and your tower."

She's right. This mysterious young man brought me a life-changing message.

I unlock my phone and text Eric.

Me: There's someone at Knitorious to see you.

Eric: Who?

Me: Jaxon Squires.

Eric: I don't know him. Work or personal?

Me: He says he's your son.

Eric: On my way.

The dog park is a ten-minute walk from here. If they run, they'll be here in five.

I place my phone on the table and take a deep, cleansing breath. *Heavy shoulders, long arms*, I remind myself, then take another deep breath. Heavy shoulders, long arms is a mantra I learned at a yoga class in my twenties. It helps release the tension in my neck and shoulders when I'm stressed.

"Are you OK, Megnificent?" April cups my cold, trembling hand in her warm, steady hand.

"A bit shaky and nauseous," I reply. "And curious. I have so many questions."

"Not as many as Eric, I bet."

April gets me a glass of water while I peek my head into the store to make sure it's not busy and Hannah can cope on her own. She's talking to a couple of knitters who are knitting in the cozy sitting area. I close the door to the store and make sure it clicks. It's difficult enough to keep anything private in this town, without having our family dramas unfold at the store during business hours.

We sit in silence, and I sip my water.

"It's been a few minutes since Jax left," April observes. "Should I check on him?"

I nod, unsure if I hope he's there or hope he had second thoughts and left.

"He's there," April confirms, closing the back door quietly. "It sounds like he's finishing his call."

I nod, both relieved and disappointed.

"Maybe we should take Jax upstairs." She gestures to the stairs that lead to the upstairs apartment. "They'll have more privacy up there."

I open my mouth to agree with April when the back-door and store door open simultaneously.

Both men enter the room at the same time. They lock eyes and freeze, stunned by the future and past versions of themselves. An eerie Twilight Zone tension fills the room.

Silence.

Oblivious to the thick fog of tension blanketing the room, Sophie trots in and breaks the silence by lapping water from her bowl, the metal tag on her collar clanging against the metal rim of the bowl. Water drips from her chin when, tail wagging, she prances over to greet me.

"Hey, Soph," I whisper, stooping down to pet her.

"You must be Jaxon." Eric speaks first.

Jax nods. "Eric?"

Eric nods and steps forward. Jax steps forward too, and they shake hands.

"Maybe you and Jax should talk upstairs," I suggest quietly to Eric.

"Good idea," April adds. "I'll take Sophie and help Hannah in the store."

"Don't you have to get back to the bakery?" I ask.

"Nope," April assures me as she walks past me to the door. "No way. Not until after." She opens the door and whistles for Sophie. They disappear into the store, closing the door behind them.

She means after I give her an update. I don't blame her. If our roles were reversed, I wouldn't leave, either.

I touch Eric's arm. He looks at me, and I take the leash and dog toy he's holding.

"If you need me, I'll be in the store." I place the leash and toy on the counter.

"Do you mind if Megan comes with us?" Eric asks, looking at Jax. "She's my partner, and I'd like her to be there."

"Sure." Jax shrugs. A micro-expression of comprehension flashes across his face, and his eyes brighten. "Wait!" He points to me and smiles. "You're my stepmum? I've never had a stepmum before."

"I've never been a stepmum before," I respond, trying but failing to match his enthusiasm.

"Does that mean the girl in the store is my sister?" he asks.

"No," I reply, shaking my head. "Hannah's father and I are divorced."

"Oh, right," Jax responds.

Eric gestures for me to go ahead of him. The three of us climb the stairs in silence except for the fourth step, which creaks when each of us steps on it.

Click here to continue reading Rest in Fleece.

ABOUT THE AUTHOR

Reagan Davis doesn't really exist. She is a pen name for the real author who lives in the suburbs of Toronto with her husband, two kids, and a menagerie of pets. When she's not planning the perfect murder, she enjoys knitting, reading, eating too much chocolate, and drinking too much Diet Coke. The author is an established knitwear designer who regularly publishes individual patterns and is a contributor to many knitting books and magazines. I'd tell you her real name, but then I'd have to kill you. (Just kidding! Sort of.)

http://www.ReaganDavis.com/

Made in the USA
Monee, IL
18 June 2021